D0392520

The Orpheus Obsession

The Orpheus Obsession

Dakota Lane

Katherine Tegen Books
An Imprint of HarperCollins*Publishers*

Printed in the United States of America. For information address HarperCollins Children's Books, a division of HarperCollins Publishers, 1350 Avenue of the Americas, New York, NY 10019.

www.harpertempest.com

Library of Congress Cataloging-in-Publication Data

Lane, Dakota.

The Orpheus obsession / Dakota Lane.— 1st ed.

p. cm.

Summary: Sixteen-year-old Anooshka Star, who has a tumultuous relationship with her mother, becomes obsessed with a rock singer and follows him into his world, and an unexpected death magnifies her troubles.

ISBN 0-06-074173-2 — ISBN 0-06-074174-0 (lib. bdg.)

[1. Love—Fiction. 2. Singers—Fiction. 3. Rock music—Fiction. 4. Family problems—Fiction. 5. Mothers and daughters—Fiction. 6. Sisters—Fiction. 7. Birds as pets—Fiction. 8. New York (N.Y.)—Fiction.] I. Title.

PZ7.L231785Or 2005   2004019106

[Fic]—dc22   CIP

                                        AC

Typography by Ali Smith

1 2 3 4 5 6 7 8 9 10

First Edition

WITH GALAXIES OF
TRUE LOVE
TO ALEX AND HAILEY

Party

01. Freedom

Just an angel, in a green disguise

—from "All Faces," © ORPHEUS XTIIMUSIC (Japan import)

Imagine having two good wings and never using them.

The first time Zack escaped, he shot out the front door, a turquoise streak headed for the dark cluster of trees across the road. That night, I woke up worrying he was dead. I lifted my window and the black spring air was soft. I sensed him out there.

So many tiny birds, in every bright color, were kept like toys in their cages, waiting for a chance to fly.

If he made it back, he'd never be locked in his cage again.

Zack was perched on the porch rail the next morning, preening, an animated spot against the green day. When he saw me, he froze and held me in his gaze. He still had something of the wild about him. And then he flew, making a neat landing on top of my head. I took him in.

02. Ecstatic Beach Trip

I saw you in the waves / you needed to be saved / maybe you were just trying / to make me feel so brave

—from "Don't Look Now," © ORPHEUS XTIIMUSIC

Moon's shovel

It's an old red Honda with a few things wrong, like Ms. ZZ Moon cannot roll her window down on the morning after my birthday, the hottest day in New York in twelve years. The broiled fumes are floating in through all the other windows and too bad for everyone else—sealed within their icy cars, oblivious to the demented beauty of real heat. We're headed to Brighton Beach.

Moon's Orpheus CD is cranked up. Not loud enough—we really have to blast it to wake up those people behind their windows.

Life is so fragile, but there are days when you discover you've climbed into your own heart and the narrow course of your veins becomes a water park joyride, flooded with a steady chemical drip from some gland in the brain, the trickle adding up to a waterfall of joy, and you just fly down that intense slide even in the presence of death and all the other drab prospects.

"You're manic today, aren't you?" says Moon, in her husky mermaid voice.

"Yeah, maybe, so what," I say. "You think I should be on medication or something?" I turn up the music.

"No," she shouts. "It's just that I can tell, that's all. I can see it in your eyes."

And I can feel it as a kind of shiny heat inside. It gives me a jangly energy, a sense of strength. Like two cappuccinos with lotsa sugar. I don't mind it a bit.

Ms. Z looks faintly like a space-age clown, with her high cheek color and her brows plucked into thin zigzags. She drives with her usual calm—her long brown foot on the gas. She hates shoes and she hates bridges. But she loves clothes! She's always got some new creation on; today it's a piece of oddly sculptable, glimmering fabric, cut that morning with a pair of scissors, wrapped around her body like a piece of origami and tied with a coarse piece of rope. That damn cutie pie. She gives off a certain delicious smell—licorice and basil, heightened in this heat.

I LOVE TO BLAST MUSIC OUT INTO THE WORLD.

Everything is festive that way.

Ma hates it, says it's tacky. When I'm back home with her, driving around our boring country roads, she forces me to keep the windows up and the stereo low. Only five or six hundred more bucks and I'll drive my own car away. Freedom, I can feel it beating through my blood already, I can feel that day in my heart like a small sun. I can see the shooting stars in the sky and the bright yellow birds flying and the gorge guys in my car on that sweet sweet day, in my own swift-flying freedom mobile when I rocket my own songs into the world.

People will snap their heads around, beaming at me and nodding in agreement with who I am. Maybe they already are, pulled in by our magnetism, mesmerized by Orpheus, with his rich, slow guitar and tribal drumming and that beautiful, echoey voice. I'm starting to like this guy. Moon always finds the best new music.

Traffic's thick but still moving, and people will be looking our way any second now. Moon and me are like magnets. But no, the shorthaired guys in their sport-mobiles keep their eyes on the road, with their hands resting on the knees of their blond girlfriends. Their windows are plastered with college stickers: CORTLAND. SUNY NEW PALTZ. BINGHAMTON. There are families and families who won't glance our way, troops of them in SUVs. We're the only ones existing in the raw element of the heat, a heat so bad it's either prehistoric or slyly futuristic. No one else on the bridge is experiencing our silver-heated reality; they're moving along, all foolish and bland within their simulated environments, oblivious behind their closed windows, not even the flick of an eye toward the one coolest girl on earth—ZZ Moon—and her sixteen-year-old cohort Anooshka Star. No recognition of my lime green heart sunglasses, served up my post-birthday morning in a glass of hand-squeezed lemonade by my sister, walking bent with a headache hangover.

Yes, I'm racing a little, but people take drugs to feel like this. Why does everything have to be a malady? I don't mind when my mind is like a pinball, jumping from thought to thought, not when all the thoughts make me happy.

Time-out for nostalgia.

"Hey Moon," I say, "remember those fat ladies on the beach with drawn-on eyebrows and coral mouth gashes and the most festive rubbery 3-D bathing caps with squiggly spikes and flowers and nubbles growing out of their heads?" Moon turns down the music a notch, looks at me and laughs.

"Yeah," she says. She's one of those drivers who use just two fingers to drive. I want to be one of those.

"And Moon, remember their matching bathing outfits and flowery thong shoes in electric citrus colors?"

"Yeah, you thought they were drag queens," says Moon.

She'd swiftly corrected me: "Idiot—they're transvestites!"

"Do you remember that time Ma hugged me?" I ask Moon, a little tug of darkness starting to bring me down. "The time the waves knocked me over?"

"I don't remember that particularly," she says. "I remember I thought you were drowning, though."

Breathing sand, blind and choking, the next wave roaring behind me, I was lifted up, not by the wave. Ma. Cooing like I was her darling baby again, whisking me to our beach blanket, fussing, wiping my face with fresh water from the thermos. ZZ Moon was looking on, her face hungry with want. Ma folded me in that sun-warmed, bathing-cap-rubber, coconut maternal-scented hug. I felt real comfort, a melting at the heart, a softening of the chest. After that, I kept getting hurt, falling down, getting sick, hoping it would happen again.

Memories, don'tcha love 'em? The salt air's setting those suckers off, firing them away like neurons.

They say you don't remember things before age three, but when I was two, there was a spot in the center of my chest connected with the outside world, specifically with people's voices. When my mother screamed at me, the spot was shredded and painful, like a scraped knee. My sister's voice soothed and brightened the spot, like honey on a sore throat.

Once it hurt so bad, I looked in the mirror, expecting to see blood. It was jarring to find nothing but smooth skin. I touched the hard bone beneath and thought perhaps that was the spot, sealed inside me long ago, like a battery. No one ever talked about that spot, so I kept it to myself.

My grandfather got me Zack for my third birthday.

"Pet store birds always die," said Ma. His first day home he had drops of blood falling from beneath his tail. "If he lives, it'll be a miracle," Ma said. That was the first time I knew about miracles. The word itself was special, like a miracle. Soon Zack was flying.

After we let him fly free, he began to sing. His songs spun a gauze around the sore spot.

A FEW MORE TOUCHING MEMORIES, ALMOST DONE.

My father would bring home animals like jackrabbits and roosters, and we would end up donating them to the petting zoo in Brighton Kiddie Park. It was a shabby little place with corny stalls based on nursery rhymes and kid stories. I did not know it was shabby at the time; it exuded a mystical glamour, as if the stories had come to life and our rejected animals could live their whole lucky lives as storybook creatures, animal starlets on display for all the excited kids pressing up against the low fences, thrusting fistfuls of animal feed into the sour, stinking pens. There were always a few pigs at the Three Little Pigs stall. They never went into their fake stone, wood, and brick houses but lay exhausted in the mud by their feeding trough. The zoo led into a big maze, the biggest garden maze on the Eastern seashore, a sign bragged. The zoo had been torn down, but the maze was still there.

I say: "Moonie, let's visit that maze. We never go there."

She just gives me a look, turns the music louder and

speeds up in the passing lane.

The center of the maze had a little round garden with tall hollyhocks and roses and three low benches facing a fishpond with green scummy water, sporting cigarette butts floating among the orange fish.

We stagger in the heat onto the crowded beach, me with my old gigantic Nikon camera, stopping every few yards to sip already warm water from our bottles.

"I think I'm going to die," says ZZ Moon.

"Just get in the water," I tell her. We barely set anything up on our towels, just hide the Nikon under a wrapped towel, strip to our bathing suits, and fling ourselves into the water. It is so, so nice. Hardly any waves, just-right coolness, everyone with such calm, happy faces. When I'm cool enough, I run back and get the camera.

I wade in, shooting Russian men with scrawny bodies and bloated stomachs next to their soft balloon wives, the men smiling their gold teeth at me. I turn the camera on these big lunk guys standing around like macho cousins, all their eyes focused on a little lunk baby at their feet waving a shovel.

I pose two giant Hispanic gay guys who speak in girlish voices, acting all sweet and shy and flattered that I want their portrait.

It's that surrealistic beach phenomenon: if you took these

people and stuck them on Thirty-fourth Street and Seventh Avenue, they would not be all smiling and nice. But here we're all happy together, letting down our stiff armor, full of trust and sweetness. It's like the rules switch for a beach and everyone suddenly knows how to behave like an advanced human.

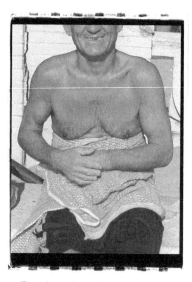

Brighton Beach guy

I have come so far. Just a year ago, I was on this same beach, wearing this stupid cheap yellow bathing suit that I was so self-conscious about. When it got wet, it became sort of transparent. I was hyper-paranoid and wouldn't go in the water.

Now—I'm wearing a normal suit and it's red and looks good and who cares, even if I were fat, even if I were flat, even if I were a quadruple D. Even if I had thick, hairy patches of pubes growing down my thighs. But I am just normal, sweaty, a person on the beach watching the litter bobbing. My sis and I jump in among the soda bottles and swim as far as the buoys, then back to the shore.

Okay, let's get hot again, says ZZ Moon. She likes to rev up her immune system by going hot, cold, hot. We lie on our beach blanket, listen to other people's music. Drop back in and splash around, lie out until we can't take it.

There is nothing like beach noise to make me feel safe. You can be annoyed by someone breathing too loudly or crumpling a potato chip bag, but then you can fall into a deep dream when blasting certain music, the stuff that's meant to be played loud. The constant noise on the beach is warm and impersonal, like the sun.

We eat at a place right on the beach with two Russian hostesses who look twelve, acting sweet as favorite nieces. Within the icy air-conditioned darkness, there is slow Russian music playing and no one there but a table of old guys drinking vodka like they're performing a scene in an HBO spy movie. We get lemony ice water, blini, and caviar. Those little eggs pop on your tongue like tear-flavor crystals, and the sour cream's slidey goodness folds into the thin, golden-edged pancakes. Heaven. Forty dollars for dinner, and ZZ Moon pays for most of it.

After, chocolate rocket bars from the Good Humor truck and back to the beach with the ice cream dripping into wrapped napkins and decorating our wrists in brown rivers. Moon picks up a discarded shovel and kneels at the water's edge, scooping out wet sand. We plop onto our stomachs, dig our toes into the sand, feeling the heat on our backs. The murmur of a hundred voices wraps around us, catlike yowls of gulls and kids piercing the haze. After a snooze we dive back into the water with humanity and the litter. Everything's working to make us feel tenderly relaxed. Finally the light becomes sharp and golden, and the sand has little cool shadows puddled in hundreds of footprint hollows. People start trekking out.

Let's go to the maze, I say.

Not that shit place, says Ms. Moon.

I love that place.

If it weren't your birthday, we wouldn't go.

But it is.

Okay, brat.

So we go.

The air's swollen with the scent of overheated roses.
Someone has turned the maze into an unexpectedly
lush garden of towering flowers in reds and purples and
nine-foot-tall sunflowers and squiggly Martian monkey
bushes. "Are we still allowed to walk in here?" I say to
ZZ Moon.

"Psycho," she says. "Hey, I'll go in the west side and
I'll race ya." She takes off running. I dive into some thick
foliage, trying for a shortcut, get my shorts stuck in the
thorny grasp of a rosebush, then run back onto the main
course, following all the little twists and turns of the narrow paths. I stop dead by a tall hedge when I hear two
guys talking.

Guy One: "This is a better angle, yeah, that's good—"

Guy Two: "Lord, it looks pretty—"

I sense my sis on the other side of the hedge. "Moon,"
I hiss, "you there?"

"Let's get out of here," she says.

I slip through the hedge. "Nah, let's check it out."

We creep forward until we're near the center of the
maze and the voices are louder. We peek through the trees.

Photo shoot in progress. Europunk photographer
behind a camera on a tripod, saying: "He's beautiful,
beautiful like that." Various stylists and assistants are
standing by admiringly, and the center of the adoration
party is a humble-looking guy, kinda short, with big,

square, black eyeglasses, a backward baseball cap, messy dark hair sticking out. He's posed against a bank of bright yellow flowers. He must be the guy who designed the garden.

Moon looks traumatized.

"What's wrong?" I say.

"Shh!" she says.

I don't see why we have to be all quiet around the hat guy. It's not a damn church. It's not like it's a movie and we're going to ruin it by talking. I leave the maze with her.

"Come on, what is it?"

Halfway out she grabs my arm.

"You know who that is, right?" She's biting her fingertips. "That guy in the hat—" I've never seen her eyes so sharp with panic. A nauseating surge of vengeance jigsaws through my gut. I'll kill him.

Then she grips me hard by the shoulders, touching her forehead to mine. "It's Orpheus," she says, in a voice so hoarse it's more of a song.

03. Magnetic Path

The light is orange /
in this overgrown garden / just before it's dark

—from "The Same," © ORPHEUS XTIIMUSIC

I see it clearly. She's a crackhead. Why else would she leave the maze when he, the guy she worships, is right in the center? That's why I, the perfectly calm one, should go back in there and ask the guy sweetly if he can give me his autograph. I happen to have a pen. And the little notebook I always bring to the city.

"I'm going," I say.

"Okay," she whispers.

Orpheus is no longer getting his picture taken.

He's sort of standing nearby while the photographer and the businessman consult. It's the perfect moment. He looks receptive to anything. I couldn't see it at first, but now I do. He is beautiful. He has dark hair, messy beneath the cap. He's exotic and almost pretty with his long lashes and curving mouth. He looks so young up close, only a little older than me. He has a sensitive face and nervous energy, bouncing from foot to foot, then absently beating out a little drum rhythm on his chest. He's in an old army green T-shirt worn thin as silk and a pair of ragged cutoffs. His limbs are long and thin but tightly muscled. He's got a real touch of the nerd, for sure: the oversize eighties specs and bright white Converse high-tops. He seems completely approachable, so I go right up. He gives me an instant, shy smile. His eyes are rare, I'm thinking. I don't even like blue eyes, but I could make an exception for his because they are *such* an unearthly, Siberian husky shade of blue, outlined in sharp black. Designer contact lenses? One more second and my staring will be pathological. "I am so sorry," I start. "But could I please ask you for your autograph? I'm really sorry if I'm intruding."

"Oh, not at all," he says. "I'm happy to." I hand him a pen and my little lined notebook opened to a blank page.

"This is really for my sister—" The words sound lame, and then I realize he's not writing but staring at my hand. "I guess I'd better use the book," he says. "Your hands seem kinda full." That's where I keep my vital notes, cell numbers, stuff like that, in waterproof pen, only partially washed away by the sea. I yank back my hand and he gives me a look, holds up his own left hand with two numbers scrawled on it. It's like we're in a happy version of that horror movie where the boy holds up his finger and says "red rum."

Orpheus draws a little bug with a baseball hat in my book. I'd rather have it there than on my hand, so I can rip it out and give it to Moon. "That's supposed to be me as a bug," he says. Suddenly he seems nervous. "I usually do a peace sign but for some reason I did this." Peace sign? Dude! Okay, the nerdiness is showing.

"It's cool!" I say. And then: "I really love your music. My sister was playing it in the car on the way here."

"Oh," he says politely. He seems available for more conversation, but I don't want to be demanding of a celebrity, especially one I know nothing about. "So is this the famous sister?"

Moon comes over, crimson faced. It's *so* cute! "Moon, Orpheus, and vice versa," I say. Like I've known the man for years.

He's wanted by his people. I thank him again since Moon obviously has a paralyzed tongue.

"Wait—," he says. For some reason this gives my heart a little jolt. He looks serious. "I didn't get your name."

I tell him.

He nods, gives a gentle wave, heads back to work.

"You are a deity!" Moon says, grabbing the book from my hand the second we're out of the maze. "This is amazing!" She kisses the buggie picture. "Orpheus is so cute! I can't believe we met him—Marley is going to freak!" Marley's her latest cavepunk, and they are in that sticky, baby-talk phase Moon gets into in the first two weeks.

Before the veil drops and she starts noticing their foreheads are too high and finding their ordinary habits intolerable. I give the poor guy until Fourth of July.

The air is still saturated with heat, and the tar of the parking lot burns as we wap the sand off our feet with towels before getting into the Honda. I glow inside from the whole day—the photos I took, meeting Orpheus—

"Shit, you could've taken his picture," ZZ Moon says.

"Right," I say. "Why didn't we think of that?"

The day is so perfect, every single part of it, that talking about it is redundant. No ends dangling, no yearning for more. Moon talks on and on, and I'm soaring inside.

But it's dusk now, and as soon as the sun sets everything will change. Like it always does, damn it.

9 P.M. on the bridge to Manhattan.

As we drive back from Brighton Beach, the sky is shiny pink and the buildings crouch against it like black dinosaurs. We drift in evening traffic on the bridge and get stuck for a few moments in front of a building outlined in violet lights. Violet, my friend Raphael always says, is the color of the nineties. There is no color for this decade because, he says, because we don't know what to call this decade. He says he would say the *o*'s but no one would know what he's talking about. A quartet of horns beep like saxophones. We pick up speed again, the air through the open windows lush as dark velvet, carrying the exotic scent of urban river, tire rubber, and coffee factories. ZZ Moon blasts Orpheus and sings along. Beneath her echoey honey voice is Orpheus, with his slo-mo drawl. The words pop out like stars, even if their meaning is obscure.

It's easy to avoid
not a box of chocolate
more an unsprung steroid
or a psychotropic rocket

I feel a spark inside, thinking of his drawing in my book like a treasure. The day worked out beautifully. There are moments when you only have to think a thought to make it happen. If only that were true at all times. You could paint your world in perfect strokes. I heard some lady in the grocery store say that the veil between this world and the other world is getting thinner.

their lilac breath engages you,
the senses interchangeable

I'm only picking up fragments of lyrics—it takes a few listens to figure out new songs. Even so, his words fit the night, my thoughts, my reality. When I'm manic like this,

I always see things moving on different tracks that correspond and go on forever, existing in a place without time. I can sometimes hear a color, see a sound. Why else would we feel emotions in our bodies? I could never explain that to anyone, and in this one simple line I feel Orpheus gets it. For a moment I have the sense of our minds, our larger minds, gently touching. It's more than that ordinary feeling a person can have when a singer captures their mood in a song. Even ZZ Moon—(singing her heart out)—does not know what I'm feeling in this car on this transcendent hot night on the bridge, tuning in to his words for the first time. It's Orpheus's mind I'm connecting to. Listening to his music in the sleek, warm air, I'm propelled into euphoria, fusing with the night. I kneel up on my seat and stick half my body out the window, letting the wind whip my face, singing into the sky until Moon yanks me back in.

04. Hungry Ghost

*You make reality more vivid / i don't know how you did it /
i had to be alone to know we were so close*

—from "Miss Bliss," © ORPHEUS XTIIMUSIC (U.K. version)

I climb into the air-conditioned bus with a sense of
relief, all sunburned and sandy, with that special clarity you
get only after being immersed in saltwater.

It's a Thursday night, so the bus is pretty quiet. I put
on my earphones, pop in my droning Japanese Koto CD,
start digging in my backpack for all my collage stuff. The
back of the bus is a good place to put together my little
photo creations.

In with my chaotic mess, Moon's slipped me the
Orpheus CD. That girl is always giving some little going-
home gift, must've tucked it in when I was getting the ticket.
I feel a spasm of guilt. Why? Because she liked him first?
Wait, who said I liked him. The music is wicked—but the
guy—who knows?

There he is on the cover of *Humanite* (she told me fifty

times it's pronounced "humanity," not "human-ite"). With that faint smile, and what is it about those eyes—a kind of warmth and shyness, a hopefulness, like a kid who has been rejected too many times to ask to play but is still holding a baseball glove, standing at the edge of the field. Okay, not that pathetic.

I play his CD so I can figure out what's behind that smile.

An hour later I haven't moved any of my photos around, cut anything out, thought of anything but the eerie way the music speaks to me. His voice has a desperate pain. I don't know why it didn't strike me so deeply in the car. The compositions are driven by the bass and deep drums, overlaid with complex mideastern horns, a bittersweet melody against the rawness of the rhythm. But the lyrics—they are peeled straight out of my most hidden thoughts. On one of the songs he speaks a kind of poem over tribal music, making the back of my neck prickle because he's describing the specific intricacies of my own life. His voice is eerily familiar and intimate as a late night talk with a friend. I play the track for the fourth time:

Sometimes I have visions of the world as fabricated,
a 3-D collage of someone's creation,
items placed here and there

people moving in a way that's sometimes random,
sometimes preordained

I take out the *Humanite* booklet again and start cutting out his face. . . .

and part of me wants to climb into this world, and
part of me wants to destroy it
but instead I just walk through it, like a visitor,
like a hungry ghost

I turn the booklet over and it says: Visit Orpheus.usa.com. This is not something I would ever do, and yet I take out my pen and write the site on my hand.

I stare into my own face in the dark mirror of the bus window. And then it hits me: the unmistakable sense of a two-way channel, put into place even before we met. I can feel him thinking about me, almost experiencing his eyes looking back instead of my own. The world has parted so quietly and immensely, exposing the thread between us. I try to go back to my collage to shake off the disorienting sensation. People make these things up all the time. Maybe I was poisoned by the sun.

My road

05. Lola Planet and the Albatross

The goldfish died / put it in the river /
make it look alive

—from "Tofu Abalone," © ORPHEUS XTIIMUSIC

Ma's passed out on the couch, her relentless Internet search for the perfect puppy still on the computer screen, showing an array of mongrels.

And then I see the puddle of water coming out from under the bathroom door—

"Damn it, Ma, again!"

INTRODUCING LOLA PLANET.

Yes, she made up her own last name and she will not say what it used to be.

So short you could think she was not my mother because I am an Amazon. Puppy, she called me when I was five and six, because I had such big feet and hands. I didn't mind; it was sweet. I have always loved endearments. Sweetheart, darling, little one, my angel. They all make my heart melt.

Sometimes she sits there with her head hunched between her shoulders and her lower lip pushed out. I want to shake her awake. I feel like she watched a film about a catatonic and is trying to impress me with her imitation. I never believe her when she acts like those women in horror movies, smiling that hard smile and saying something demented like: "Anooshka Star Girl, do you sometimes feel like you have the hard beginnings of horns growing out of the top of your head? Is your throat itching? Do you have a heat inside you that only ends when you have sex?" She knows I haven't had sex. (Okay, once, with Sean, but she doesn't know about that and I try to forget it.)

Unlike most of my friends' mothers, she doesn't care that I'm waiting for someone who really loves me. She's not concerned that I'm waiting too long, maybe repressing my healthy desires out of some kind of fear. She usually skims right over every major turning point of my life. Either that or gets hyper-involved. Asking a million questions, all the wrong ones.

"Anooshka, have you finished your report on the atomic particle theory?"

"No, Ma, it's not a report, it's a test with an essay, and I took it two days ago, and it was on string theory."

"Oh, whatever," she says. "At least I take an interest in you. Someday when I'm dead from leukemia, you'll regret being such a hideous brat."

I used to feel guilty from her threats, but it was nothing compared to the way I went into a form of shock when she would lock herself in the bathroom and loudly proclaim her intent to kill herself. I remember helping Moon to get a ladder out of the garage to try to scale the outside wall when we were like five and nine years old. We almost killed ourselves climbing the ladder, and in the end our father came back and broke down the door and Ma had just nicked her wrist with a disposable razor. It twisted my gut to see the rusty-colored scratches on her wrist. I remember hugging her as tight as I could and kissing her so many times on the cheek that she finally told me to stop.

Now when she mentions her impending death, I sometimes think: Go for it! I tend to clam up and she hates that.

She blames it on my uneven genius. "Oh, there's your developmental disorder acting up again," she says. "You should eat more fish oil. Your brain would work better. You would be able to respond to me when I'm talking to you. You could be more in touch with your feelings instead of being *so damn rude*!"

She stamps off, her exaggerated show of anger making her look like a spoiled kid. I feel satisfied at remaining calm. On to the next thing. Mostly the situation is barely tolerable. I've always fantasized about calling the child abuse hotline.

Ah, Ma, gotta love her. Just not right this second, cleaning up her mess.

I get to work on the flood first—mop, bucket, heaps of towels. Then I try shaking her awake:

"You did it again, Ma—the tub—the floor's going to rot!"

She gives me a bleary smile. "Hi babe . . . Oh, I was so depressed, I slept all day—I thought I'd take a bath to cheer myself up—"

"Yeah, whatever, go to bed."

Ma shuffles off with that naughty, self-indulgent, barely chastened child look. I go to turn off the computer, muttering to myself like I'm the one on Ward D. "How was your weekend, Anooshka? Anything fun happen? How's your sister? How on earth did you keep cool during the heat wave; the city must've been a bitch—"

"Are you sure you want to shut down?" says the computer in a robotic Swedish accent.

Suddenly I'm typing in Orpheus.usa.com.

The site bursts on with an electric background and a big *O*, with the opening notes from one of his songs.

I don't even sit down, because I'm not really doing this. I click on the *O* and it turns into a home page with Pictures of Orpheus and icons to the left, indicating Diaries, News, Concerts, Fan Site. I click on Diaries and a list of recent ones comes into view; he has one for almost every day from the past few weeks. The one at the top of the list—June 16—has a blinking legend next to it: Just Written. I click on this, feeling like a spy.

Orpheus Online
New York

someone told me that when the addictions and
obsessions kick in to just picture a dead
albatross around your neck . . .

I can see him walking down a street, a prehistoric dead bird draped around his neck. He's furtive and edgy, hands in pockets. Hollow-eyed medieval characters peer out from darkened doorways.

. . . and you say to yourself . . . oh yes, here's
that albatross again . . . what an annoyance, but
it'll be gone in a few days. . . .

I'm on that street with him now, and we're standing face-to-face and he's gripping my shoulders, looking into my eyes.

. . . do you even know what i mean?

06. Like Morphine

Half-sparked / pardon my heart / i could download
your thoughts / by the swings in the dark

—from "Mercy," © ORPHEUS XTIIMUSIC

**It's morning, quiet. Buttery light falling into the house,
the crystal fluting of birds,** warm earth scent drifting
through the open windows. Not a computer day. Go outside and lie on the prickly new grass in the backyard, face
to the sun, leaves quietly shifting above. Crows barking
back and forth. I won't go inside. Won't sit in front of the
computer. Won't go online.

Orpheus Online
New York
fishlove

am I the only one who watched America's Hilarious Videos
tonight and saw a little girl sobbing as she tried to give her
beloved fish a flushed funeral? She said that for two whole
weeks he had been the best fish she had ever known. She

snatched him back in her chubby fist just as the toilet began to flush. i can understand how two weeks can seem like forever. bonding is bonding.

yes, i just admitted to watching tv at 8 p.m. on a fri. night. but i was also eating a bag of cilantro Thai chips, and talking to durgha (on my new cell). i'm working on a theory that multitasking gives you ADD and not vice versa.

now the sun is turning the sky an acid orange. time for bed. sleep tight.

orpheus

If I hadn't met him, I would probably imagine a much older guy writing. When I look at him on the CD cover and think of him in person—those arms with the long, ropy muscles, the quick smile, and those exotic eyes—I get an echoey thrill. It really happened. We met. We had that ethereal connection. It's still there, that mutual pull. I reach for the phone to call Raphael and Agnes—but not yet.

The day's grown dreary. I'm up in my loft bed, staring into my laptop, Zack singing into his own face, perched on the thin frame of my mirror. I can see myself in the mirror, hunched over the screen, still in my pj's. I feel vaguely guilty. But it's summer, it's going to rain, I can do what I want. I turn up his music, wondering if the CD will wear out and die. Ma's still at the gym. Thank God. She's so much better when she works out.

In some ways, Moon's right. Ma's improved since we were young. She used to lose important items—bills, keys, envelopes full of money, a vital phone number on a scrap of paper. And then—watch out! Moonie and I would immediately be blamed, either for intentionally hiding the item or for distracting her so much that we caused her to lose it. Entire days could be ruined, spent searching for the item. We would become literal prisoners of the house and her madness until she found the item or let it go.

The worst time was when she was missing a bottle of mood pills she'd just gotten from the pharmacy. As the saga around the pills progressed, she became increasingly threatening. She promised to scream at us if the pills were found that first day, to punish us if they were found within the week, and to beat us if they took a month to be found. Weeks passed and no pills. (Moon and I talked about the big flaw in her reasoning: why would we steal something that would improve her mood?)

One afternoon Ma and I were standing on high stools in the kitchen; I was helping her to clean a window. Without warning, she smacked me full in the face, knocking me to the ground. I was crying, asking her why.

"Because I know you took the pills," she said.

I was ten the last time she hit me. The smack left a long-lasting purple crescent, which may have triggered some remorse—or fear of what the neighbors would think. Moon, who was fourteen, told Ma that if she ever touched me again, she would ram her fist down Ma's throat.

I started writing on my hand that week, tiny-lettered incantations like: STAYAWAYFROMME. My hands have never been naked since.

MY SISTER WAS ME MUDDER.

My sister Zoetrope Zallulah Moon had the worst of it. She's four years older, and she was carrying me around and changing me when I was a baby. Ma used to get back into bed first thing in the morning and stay there all day. It was a good place for her.

When she was mobile, she'd whack us in the face, saying we were staring or laughing at her. Then, when we cried, she had this little trick of crawling around on the floor imitating us. The kitchen had a linoleum floor from the 1950s, with a jazzy, abstract geometric pattern of amorphic shapes in pea green and brown gold, overlaid with tiny red squares.

I remember screaming down onto the floor, the hardness and gritty feeling of the dirty floor, cold on my palms and bare knees, the battery in my chest connected to the little red squares and the blatant spectacle of my mother on the floor with me screaming, her face enormous. Her mouth was a flapping cave, and a feeling of wrongness tore into me like an ambulance. And then I was lifted up and held against something soft and yellow and kissed on the head. This was my sister, blocking off the red squares.

My sister is jealous. These days, Moon thinks I'm having the divine teenage years she missed out on. She somehow believes that our mother is cured, and she was the one who took all the hell. She doesn't realize that hell is being alone with Ma.

But Ma's out of the house for the moment, and I can blast my CD. When you put together his CD with his diaries, there are two Orpheuses—one a genius and the other this guy having his mundane routines like the rest of us. I could easily see him eating those chips, talking to that Durgha person, getting teary over the girl and the fish. Maybe he was being sarcastic. Weird that he just fast-forwarded from watching TV to hours after, sun rising and time for bed. What kind of crazy stuff did he do all night? Wild parties or more TV and chips? Maybe he's an insomniac.

He didn't mention anything about meeting a girl in the middle of a maze in Brighton Beach. He gives out tons of autographs every day, no big deal.

I climb down from the loft and stare out my bedroom window into the rain. Green gloom. The big old willow tree all glistening and drippy. A rusty pickup truck goes by; we're so close to the road, I can feel the vibrations in my fingertips on the windowsill. The wet afternoon is so green it glows, rain falling in sharp points into the river across the street.

I'm thinking: I'm starting my day, and Orpheus went to sleep only three hours ago. It's weird to be that tuned in to a stranger's schedule.

Zack, who's been watching me from the bed, flutters down to my shoulder. I put him on my hand, his little feet curling around my index finger. I squeak to him in my bird squeak. He cocks his head, lets out the cutest chirp, and then just starts singing to me. He has a faraway look in his eyes when he sings. He's into Orpheus. He's crazy for strong drums; they juice him up.

Doesn't he make you psycho sometimes, my gorgeous boy pal Raphael asked me back when we were studying for finals and Zack was singing his heart out. No, never. It's like having your own cartoon come to life. Zack just catches the mood and goes with it. He draws joy into the room.

That is so pretty, Zack, I tell him. He focuses on me. A telepathic empathy passes between us, built on so many years of silent understanding.

Best eye contact for a bird award.

That's what Raphael gave him last year. I raise Zack gently to my face and rub my nose delicately on his chest. An exercise of mutual trust. He has occasionally given in and bitten my nose. He smells divine, a perfume of sunflowers and warm blue feathers. I begin to climb up to my loft bed again, awkwardly using one hand because Zack's perched on my other, when I remember he can fly. "No free rides, lazy boy!" I tell him, gently shaking him off.

No one knows about the Orpheus fascination. I'm dying to tell Raphael, but he will completely tear me up about my taste in music. He hates electronic stuff. He's into the new basics—guitar and voice and harmonica. Boring. But when I play him this CD, he will get how cool the lyrics are and he will get Orpheus's sexy voice.

Okay, it is sexy. Not obvious sexy like all deep and raspy, but sexy because there's a sweetness and a faint sadness that makes you want to listen carefully, like when someone whispers. I've got the CD player on automatic, so I've heard the whole thing three times since I woke up. Bliss. Alone on a Saturday. Rain. This music. *If only his diaries were as powerful as his music.* I keep getting off the bed to move around my room to that edgy, funky guitar groove and that fantastic beat.

> *the hideous beauty of fish,*
> *when they're left too long in the cave,*

just close your eyes you say,
that's how you remind me to be calm

I search the site and find Orpheus's very first diary from last year:

Orpheus Online
New York

maybe, like all the other good music stars, i should be a little more secretive. nah, i can't help it if i'm chatty, and if you want to talk back, we have the message boards and you can post anything you like. chances are some night when i can't sleep and there are no more cosby reruns on, i'll read it.

orpheus

How to Make a 3-D Collage
Wait until it rains and turn off your computer. (Unless you want to make a cyber collage, but that's another story.) Get all the cool stuff you've been saving, that poster you peeled off the wall in the city, scraps from magazines, the picture of Moon's place with the sun mysteriously casting stars on the side of the building, that Japanese candy wrapper you found on the

ground, and of course the five hundred pics of your pals and enemies and the strangers whose images you like to steal so you can turn them into the members of a fictional tribe. Make sure you've got lotsa ordinary stuff like buildings and trees, and then you start gluing the stuff all together on stiff cardboard and bend it this way and that so it stands up and pretty soon you have this whole surrealistic village that you've been doing since you were eight, and Zack picks through it, making the tiny, thin cutouts fly up but you don't get mad. In fact, you don't even finish cutting out that pic of Orpheus from his CD cover because you'd rather go back online than glue his head onto that fish riding the bicycle through the ill-conceived, half-finished, psychedelic suburban neighborhood.

Why can't I stop reading his stuff? Just a few more. Zack seems bored, looking like a guy with his hands in his pockets, pecking at imaginary seed. I walk away from my collage village for now, reading a diary from just a few days ago.

Orpheus Online
ten-mile cure

it doesn't make it easy realizing that more than half this world is at this moment operating under some sort of delusion or trance . . . and it doesn't help that even when you're in the thick of the delusion, or especially when you are, that sometimes the one you are deluded about appears before you in real life and looks you in the eyes and smiles and it goes into your brain like morphine.

how do you deal with your demons?

i will probably eat a whole box of that salty salty licorice that comes from holland.

and then take a massive walk across the brooklyn bridge. After that I might play a little on the old banjo. It's humanly impossible to be obsessed and play the banjo at the same time.

orpheus

Go Orpheus, drama! We like drama. *But who was he obsessed with?* And how could he announce to the world that he was going walking on the bridge? Tons of fans would ambush him and so much for his lonely walk. He must've written this and then gone out at four A.M., and then posted it when he got back. Now I'm thinking like a cop. Suspect left house at four A.M. I flash on him sleeping again, in the middle of the day. People are probably more receptive to your psychic messages when they're uncon-scious. God, I'm demented.

I check the boards to see if his fans posted anything in reaction. If anyone tried to find him on the bridge or if this diary triggered a flurry of discussions about obsessions and addictions. The postings were completely moronic, written by seven year olds.

> Bluedreamer: Orpheus, if u are reading this, do you remember me from the show in Chicago where I was waiting in your hotel lobby for like 20 hours with my friend Tessa and you let us take two pictures. I was wearing cowboy boots. You were SO nice.

> LAXLISA: Never mind the puppy love, did anyone else have an orgasm from that vocal loop on the Illuminate song?

> queencentral: have u no shame? (looms imperiously over LAXLISA) And your mascara is running—as usual!

I am so lame, it took me about three years to figure out how people could put actions into their e-mails. Any time I went online and tried to follow a loop in a chat room, it seemed like everyone was in on this special game. I kept picturing all these twenty-year-old guys pretending to be young girls.

If I were to go online and post a message about meeting

Orpheus in the maze, I would be just like everyone else. I sign off and close my eyes.

Flashing brightly inside me, the connection again. That twinge of the mystical, that gentle beckoning. I feel his loneliness pressed softly into my chest. If I could just smile at him and have it go into his brain like morphine.

The wind rises outside and the rain suddenly grows stronger. I can almost feel his sleeping form.

07. Zing!

Rainbows are obvious until you see one /
all i want is your snapshots from hell

—from "Baghdad Zoo," © ORPHEUS XTIIMUSIC
with Manouche Toyashi

ANOOSHKA'S ISLAND—DAY

A deep blue sky, one cloud drifting. We move lazily across the sky and then down and down, taking in the lush, wild surroundings of ANOOSHKA's secret island in the middle of the river: a tiny outcropping of purple and yellow flowers shielded by tough saplings. The river's rushing audibly, and ANOOSHKA's lying on her favorite flat rock. We take in her fingers trailing in the water, her bare legs, T-shirt rolled up, belly bared to the sun, her HUGE SUNGLASSES.

While holding on her absolutely still BODY, we hear crackling noises through the brush, twigs breaking. A SHADOW falls over her. She doesn't move. DROPS of water start dripping onto her belly from an unknown source.

SUDDENLY her hand lashes out like a snake and grips the wrist of RAPHAEL, who's standing over her, grinning. He's BEAUTIFUL, tall and big, dressed in a torn work shirt and cutoffs. She gets to her feet in a fluid karate pose and puts him in a sort of lock.

ANOOSHKA: No matter what you say, I'm not going to that party, and neither are you!

My life as a movie. Too bad it snaps back into reality. We pass the afternoon at my secret river spot and next thing you know, it's early evening and we're roaring around the curvy river road in Raphael's mud-spattered jeep. I have my feet propped on the dashboard and am painting my toenails apricot—delicate operation.

It's not quite dark, and it's hot in the way that you can smell whiffs of backyard barbecues and have clear fantasies of being twenty-three and being continually at summer parties with a few normal, constantly joking people, a sense of wholesomeness and profound hope settling around you because there is a perfect lack of humidity in the hot blue air and your heart swells rather than your brain matter.

The top is off. We're blasting electronic French tango music. Vah-room-bah! Bah! BAH! Tick, tock, tock, TOCK! I notice a stray black hair growing by my ankle bone. Damn! I just shaved this morning. Hate when you miss those pesky hairs. I try to trap it with my thumb and forefinger to pluck it out.

Raphael takes in my grooming activity and gives me a whatever, dude look. "So I guess you're an official stalker now," he shouts above the engine and the careening music.

I punch his arm.

"Hey, don't attack the driver!" He is so cute with his thin plastic turquoise eyeglasses. Yeah, I finally had to tell my people. What's the point if you don't tell your people? Who else can bring you down like they do?

"Why does everyone think I'm a stalker?" I prop my feet out the window to let the polish dry. "I'm not sure I even like the dude."

"Oh, that's why you go online every day and you're the president of his fan club!"

"There isn't a club—I just looked at his diaries because he's so—"

He gives me the giant, all-knowing Raphael smile. "Yes, Anooshka? Because he's what—a lonely but inspiring genius? A cutting-edge pop star exploring himself endlessly?"

I turn my face to the soft, kind sun.

It's great hanging out with someone you know so well.

First time I saw him, Raphael was four years old and licking a massive green lollipop in the preschool parking lot and was I pissed! I was not even allowed to wear anything that brightly colored. My mother's theory—bright colors equal mental illness.

And—eating it in the morning! His parents were perfect. *So* nice, so friendly, so relaxed, with open, cheerful faces. A Jewish and black mother and a Tibetan father. Nice combo, right?

Oh yes, Raphael is *gorge*. Even as a baby boy, with that golden skin and straight, bamboo amber hair and those glowing eyes. He had a soft illumination around his whole face.

Fast-forward to sixth grade. We lived next to each other and became best friends. He was my photography model. (Even cross-dressed for me a few times.) We raised lop-eared rabbits and entered them in the county fair. Made new trails in the woods with our bikes. Were obsessed with eighties sitcoms. People thought we were having sex! We didn't even kiss. Okay, once we tried, but it was weird so we stopped, and that was four years ago. He was the one I first told when I got my period. When he moved ten miles away, we stayed best friends. I love him like crazy, man. He is my angel.

I'm shooting pictures out the window with my tiny old silver Olympus. Blurred greenery looming above low stone walls on the right. Stand up and brace myself with one hand on the seat to shoot the cascading storybook river on Raphael's side. Turn around to get the splatted animal on the road. Chartreuse moss on an old barn roof spotlit by sudden sun. That is a boring shot; I would rather get a Danish model waking up with puffy eyes and a bleak expression, staggering out to check her mailbox. Zing! Surprise!

"So you want to go to the party or not?" says Raph.

There's always a party somewhere, always a place where a parent is gone for at least half the night. This one's at Lindsay Baker's dad's place in Woodstock. The ones at her house sometimes get wild, but you also have to deal with a certain revolting group, aka my old friends.

The pre-sunset yearning is about to hit. I know what's ahead: going home, the gloom gathering in the house, the air cooling outside. Zack flying in panicked, squawking circles until a light is turned on. Probably nothing cooking on the stove, have to grab something unappetizing out of the moth-smelling food closet like Ramen soup or mac and cheese. Ma will be in the dark, hunched in for the night with some phantom Internet assignment. Everything would feel so much happier if I knew there was a shower, a change of clothes, and a big social event in the near future.

"But it won't be fun," I say.

"Who says fun is the ultimate experience?" he says.

I point my camera at Raphael. *Click. Click. Click.* I'll go, I tell him.

08. Scarlett at the Party

And i see the stars, and so what,
they're okay / and i see the stars even if you don't
and i stare / coz i see the stars, they mean a lot /
you don't care / you're down there / busy looking hot

—from "Startoon," © ORPHEUS XTIIMUSIC

DAMN, I'M GOOD.

She's there, folded into her Japanese robe, small face staring into the cold light of her computer.

"Oh good," Ma says. "I want to show you this puppy." I click on a lamp, and she peers at me startled, eyes ghoulish, yesterday's makeup pooled into shallow canyons. Deep sleep creases are smushed into her cheek like she spent the day in bed.

"Hey, this reminds me of LoveMatch," I tell her. "Dogs instead of guys." Whoops. Instant traumatic response.

"Thank you, Anooshka." She swipes at an unruly piece of hair and it's coated with so much product, it ends up sticking out at an odd angle. She looks like an aging goth rocker with her raccoon eyes and whacko hair. "Thank you for shitting on my enthusiasms."

AH, YES, THAT'S ME.

First I stood by patiently all winter while she obsessively looked up weirdos on LoveMatch.com, aka Psychos Anonymous. After that, she roamed the Internet for used cars. Once she forced me to stop studying for a final to look at a ten-thousand-dollar pink Thunderbird that someone was selling in Florida. We were not going to Florida. We did not have ten thousand dollars. We didn't even need a car. She acts like she's investigating some life and death thing, like it's her job. In a way it is her job. She gets disability for being totally dysfunctional and then every day proves that she is.

"Ma, I just don't know if we should get a dog." I force myself to sound neutral.

"This is not about we, Anooshka. And you can drop that patronizing, pitying attitude. Besides, you always wanted a puppy. You begged me to get one."

"Yeah, when I was like six."

"It's for me, anyway. I know I'm going to be the one taking care of him."

She clicks on one of the mongrels and the screen fills with a pic of a fuzzy, bearlike creature.

"He looks really young."

"Eight weeks. I want a puppy. I want that experience." She lifts her chin. I *am* going to win that twenty-four-meter race, even if I did lose the leg last summer.

"So Ma, I'm going to this party tonight at Lindsay Baker's house . . . probably about eight, with Raphael."

"What do you mean you're going? Since when did you stop asking and start telling me about your plans?" she says. "That is just not acceptable."

Her nostrils always get a little flare when she gets angry. I'm zeroing in on ugly details to avoid reality.

"Okay then." I can do this. Someday I will be gone. She is only a little, little mother. "Can—I—go—to—the—party—at—Lindsay's—tonight?"

"No, Anooshka, you can't. Not tonight."

"What?" I feel my face grow hot. "You are kidding me!"

"No, sweetie, you've been out every night this week and—"

"It's summer, Ma. I'm sixteen. What am I supposed to do—stay home with you—"

"The way you say that—like it's some kind of hell—"

"It is!" I'm blowing it, but she is just so amazingly crazed. I swipe at the idiotic tears racing down my cheeks. "It's not like I drink, I don't smoke pot, I'm not a slut—why are you punishing me?"

"Fine, Anooshka, go to your party but next time you need something don't ask me!" She wags her finger at me.

"And I mean that!" She turns dramatically back to her computer.

I pound upstairs to my room, muttering "psycho" under my breath.

"And I heard that!"

Urgent business: gotta find an outfit.

There's a subdued squeak—Zack huddled on the top of my open door.

"Oh Zack, this is a terrible spot for you," I tell him. "I could have closed the door and killed you." Zack has too much fun outside his cage and hardly ever makes it back there before dark. He ends up stuck in the oddest places, helplessly waiting for my return.

"I'm so sorry, sweetie." He ducks his head and gives me his humble look. He lets out a purring sound like a miniature dove. He gives me a forgiving blink. I ease my finger under his little curling feet and bring him to his cage. He climbs inside and eats like a starved man. Why do they say people eat like birds when birds eat like pigs?

Phone.

It's ZZ Moon.

I don't pick up.

How do I know it's ZZ Moon? (And no caller ID, of course.)

I just know.

I always know.

The air around the phone becomes ZZ Moon air. No other way to explain.

Why do I not pick up? Why do I stand in the middle of the room with my arms folded staring at the phone?

Because we will fight. About Ma.

Okay, I pick it up.

Hello, blah blah. Yes, hello, blah blah. Three seconds of blah later and we are at it.

"It wouldn't kill you to be nicer to her. At least Ma cares about you and wants to spend time with you. She didn't care if I was out shooting up or whatever."

How many times have we had this exact fight?

Nine hundred eighteen.

She takes Ma's side. She makes me feel guilty because Ma was a worse mother to her. She spent all those years taking care of Ma and now she thinks it's my turn. I have other ideas.

OKAY, THEN!

YEAH, OKAY, LATER!

Bad feelings through the wires.

Put the phone down.

Blast Orpheus.

Turn my shower on so it'll be good and hot.

Begin throwing possible party outfits onto the bed.

COME DOWNSTAIRS AROUND 7:30 P.M.

I'm fresh washed, smelling like a green flower, a sublime new Ms. Thang. New mood happening here. The madre factor has mellow Morcheeba playing. Tibetan incense burning. Ma in well-lit kitchen.

"Anoo, babe, can you set the table for us?"

"Sure, Ma." Come up next to her at the stove. Put arm across her shoulders, lean my head against hers. "Wow, that looks awesome."

Crisp squares of tofu and jasmine rice and some lemongrass coconut sauce simmering. "I can't believe you made this so quickly."

"Yes, I am amazing."

See, we don't need big discussions to restore our sanity. We are happy together again. My ma, I love her. Not crazy, but quirky. And why shouldn't she have a cute little puppy bear to keep her company?

We eat with a few candles. Her sleep lines have faded and her face is shiny clean. Her hair still sticks out, but now it looks cool.

I tell her how delicious the food is. I thank her for cooking. I clean our dishes and put away the leftovers.

"You look really cute tonight, by the way," she calls from the computer. I don't know why she's on that thing now that she has found the pooch. Perhaps looking for last-minute ones? Better not to know.

Maybe she's finally writing her long-lost novel about her years as a punk rock drummer. "You do have a bit too much lipstick on," she says. "You might want to blot it a little. Just tone down that shine a bit."

Raphael, my hero, beeps outside.

The pool is one of those faux cliff and waterfall deals, like a mermaid's grotto, nicely done with lots of money. Lit well enough to see that some of the girls are dancing topless to trip-hop music. People are smoking pot. A girl draws the letters $X \ldots T \ldots C \ldots$ on a guy's bare thigh in Magic Marker. The food table is piled with pizzas, chips and chocolate cakes that have been grabbed more than cut. Bottles of every type of booze, all top shelf. The house is a football field away, up on a hill, but the music is so loud the vodka bottle on the table is vibrating.

There's an idiot couple hooking up in the pool and they're annoying, but we're in no rush to go back into the house.

"Maybe I shouldn't have done it," Agnes wails, patting her short, loosely curled Afro. She chopped off her foot-long dreads at the beginning of the summer. "I feel like I'm neutered. And this thing—doesn't it make me look like a cult leader?" She also just got a tiny red symbol tattooed behind her ear. She dreamed about the symbol one night. (Agnes is an absolute dream freak; we've stopped telling her our dreams because she analyzes them to pieces.)

I remind her of this. "What's more important, being true to your dreams or not looking like a cult leader?"

Someone's left a fashion mag on the poolside table, so I grab it and start looking for this one chick who kinda

At the party

looks like her, only Agnes has more class. This insecure stuff has got to end, because Agnes is amazing. (And her new vanity is driving me nuts!)

We come to a lovely two-page spread of Scarlett crawling half nude on the floor, in a micro-mini that's swaddled around her like a diaper. We stare at it for a few beats. They were all talking about it before, and here it is in all its sordid glory.

"She's just such a bitch," Agnes says.

"Maybe we're just jealous," I say.

"Of what—being in a Glorious Johnson video? Debasing yourself in a diaper?"

"Meow," says Raph.

"Oh, come on," I tell him. "Don't you wish your life would just change like—*ding*—in an instant?"

Scarlett's seventeen and she's been coming up to Woodstock every summer since she was six. Her career took off two years ago. First she starred in a few TV commercials for Sunburst gum. Then she danced in a Racing Albinos video. This year she's the print model for GlamRockCandy makeup and has her face all over Manhattan buses with her pierced tongue sticking out. She shows up in the *Daily News* gossip column and appears in *People* magazine shopping for boots with Paris Hilton. And if you don't happen to read those publications, she lets you know where she's been.

"Yeah, she did kinda have a flabby persona before," Raph admits.

In elementary school Scarlett was dull and blobbish, with round, slouchy shoulders and flat brown hair hanging in her face. She wore glasses and they were always smudged. She had the kind of postnasal bad breath that smells like burned plastic and sour milk. She had a nervous cough and she wore dumb clothes. And then she showed up one summer with her hair dyed platinum. She'd lost weight, gotten taller, and sprouted breasts. Suddenly she was cool. And even though she'd never been all that warm and cuddly, she was now authentically bitchy.

The couple's actually doing it in the pool now, so we head up to the house, past the kids in the hot tub, past the kids bouncing drunk on the trampoline. That would be a nice newspaper headline.

We stop to sneer-lust at Lindsay's metallic pink Hummer in the driveway (four full months before her sixteenth birthday). She's okay even if she is Scarlett's best friend from birth and one of those short girls with really big boobs and a great attitude so all the guys think she's hot even though she isn't really pretty at all. Okay, we are jealous.

Nowhere in sight. That's where Lindsay's parents are. They divorced and they both believe in giving kids freedom and they are both somewhere else for the entire night. And this happens *all* the time.

Lindsay's dad has a recording studio and he's got all these gold records and Polaroids of superstars. I've seen them a million times, but for some reason they still fascinate me and I stop to look at them in the entrance hall now—zooming in on one with Lindsay and Scarlett in their pj's, posed with the lead guy from Second Skin. You can tell the dad had the stars over and made them pose for pics at breakfast.

We keep moving, through a cluster of kronked kids, flicking their cigarette ashes on the floor, drinks sloshing onto the rug, hands all slipping down each other's bathing suit bottoms, drunk dancing.

And here's Scarlett, draped on the edge of a fat leopard couch, cuddled next to Lindsay and the flamboyant Ian, who's using Scarlett's thigh as a footrest for his snakeskin boot. Scarlett looks at us with her bleary, stoned, reptile eyes and flashes a fraction of unveiled lust in Raph's direction. He, of course, is oblivious, but I catch the vibe and she catches me catching it.

"So I guess gay is the new black?" Scarlett's annoying faux-bored voice cuts through the party atmosphere like peach room spray. Whoops. Her little barb, directed at Raph, doubly cuts Agnes. Scarlett looks embarrassed and then decides to go for defiant, with a little lift of her chin. Agnes stares her down. I'm about to say something to the queen bitch but then Ian does it for me: "Just 'cause you don't have a magic wand, girl, don't mean she don't."

People sometimes think Raph is gay because he is so

damn gorgeous and dresses so divinely weird. Tonight: lime overalls, torn white T, checked cap. An anti-look. He also smells like candy. Scarlett, who has a face like a starved cat, thinks he is my boyfriend.

The starved feline look is enhanced with purple eyebrows drawn on in straight lines, glossy blond hair chopped above her ears, and pink metallic false eyelashes. She is wearing a perfect simple stretchy black dress and no stockings or shoes on her six-mile-long legs. Her forehead is so high that it looks like she shaved part of her hairline. Her nose is slightly wide and is the whole reason she never made it as a supermodel, or so the rumor goes, as if I care.

Ian is cool to intervene. Guess he remembers the time I let him copy my notes in science, circa eighth grade. Handy growing up with these people.

Meanwhile it would be Agnes who has the wand, if Raph was gay, because Agnes is the one who would—but he's not—and I'm—oh, forget it.

Raphael doesn't care either way; he wiggles his hands in front of Scarlett's face like he's putting a voodoo spell on her and then just walks away cracking up. Scarlett probably thinks it's a mating dance.

We move deeper into the smoky party room of Lindsay's dad's amazing guest house in Woodstock. It's got a recording studio upstairs and it's made out of rough-hewn planks and smells like pine trees and woodsmoke, and currently of joints. We make our way to the drink table in the game room, which has a pool table and vintage video games, and tons of couches set up facing a six-foot TV screen. I see Sean, dressed in his fake punk ensemble, guzzling a beer, studiously avoiding eye contact. So what. When I see someone in those studded collars from the mall, I just want to strip them buck naked and throw them to some London skinheads. And Sean is the worst kind of offender, in his red and black getup with his newly spiked and dyed hair. Keep moving, moving.

10:30 P.M. Blazed, high, tripping on XTC. What half the kids are.

11 P.M. Drunk, obliterated, wrecked. What most of the kids are. Even more couples are supposedly out having sex in the pool. I am not that interested in swimming; I don't care what chlorine kills. Agnes went home; Raph and I are just masochists. We're parked in front of Ms. Pac-Man and I just got the high score of 180,000 points.

It might help if I could drink, but I can't since that Evil Time of too much tequila—(I can hardly say that word without gagging; why is it always tequila?)—and too much Sean at New Year's.

Luckily Raphael hates being high on anything.

Without him, I'd probably feel like I'm on acid just by observing the lively antics of people who are high.

Like now, for example. Two guys are wrestling right in front of us like massive, yowling, grunting two year olds. They look stupid. They are stupid. The activity should last like two minutes, but it's been going on for at least twenty because they're high and they don't care that they look like clonking, rolling cavemen.

"Where's Agnes when we need her!" moans Raphael. He's been liking her lately.

I remind him that her masochistic threshold is lower than ours.

"Don't you mean higher?"

"Do you like her or don't you?" I say.

"Yeah, don't you?"

I can't resist: "You just better not drop me if you guys really hook up."

Midnight. Lindsay is doing a bizarre chickenhead lap dance thing in front of two guys who keep telling her to move so they can see the TV. Scarlett is dancing with another skinny model girl and every so often they kiss and some of the guys are acting like freaks about it and other people are pretending that it's cool and they're cool with it but they keep staring anyway.

Five or six kids took E, even though earlier people were saying everyone took it. You can tell who's on it because their faces look like melted cartoon characters. They are all red and sweaty and sorta unfocused looking, and they have these giant idiot grins. They keep walking around together in little clusters, popping in and out of the house as if they are on some sort of mission where nothing is ever accomplished.

If Lindsay's parties are so dumb, how dumb does that make us for coming to them?

Raphael reminds me to whip out the camera. People are basically too too whacked to care if I'm shooting. I get some really crucial ones of these girls jumping outside on the trampoline. And these completely wild ones by the torches outside. These shots look like the kids are in the caverns of hell, sudden flickers of red light on writhing flesh. *Clickety-click.*

1:00 A.M. I'm up on the kitchen counter and Raph's digging in the fridge when Sean comes in and slides up right next to me, breathing on me. I try to ignore him, then I start to hop off the counter—and he blocks me.

He starts singing a pop lyric: "We can do it again . . . you just tell me wh-hen. . . ."

"Uh, Raph?" I say.

Sean's already scooting out of the kitchen.

"Ooo, sca-wee," says Scarlett, who's standing, a bit unstable, in the kitchen doorway. "Macho boy," she tells Raph. Then to me: "Why don't you like Sean, anyway? He said you did him once, and—"

"You really are a bitch," Raph tells her. I start pulling him out of the room. She isn't worth it.

"Are you saving your second time for Orpheus?"

I snap to. "What are you talking about?"

"I heard you're having a thing—"

"You're insane."

"It's okay, I'm done with him, not a problem!" Scarlett comes in close enough for me to smell her boozy breath and expensive perfume. "He's fun and he'll like you for at least two weeks! In your case, maybe one, but—it'll be a really good week."

"Fuck off," I tell her. "Go take your lithium."

1:15 A.M.

Wrapped in a blanket in Raph's jeep, wind whipping my hair. The crickets are on cocaine. Raph's okay if you can deal with his Zen silences. He's humming to himself, tapping out a rhythm on the steering wheel. He'll probably go home and play guitar until the sun comes up.

"Did she really go out with him?"

He comes back to reality with a start. "Who?"

"Scarlett and—ah, never mind."

He gives a professional nod, like a doctor satisfied with his own diagnosis. "Somebody's got it bad."

1:30 A.M.

I will not go online. I will not listen to the Orpheus CD.

1:35 A.M.

I put earphones in and mute the computer so Ma's Doberman ears do not wake up. First I read a whole page of him apologizing to his fans because his concert next weekend is already sold out. (A little bit of a brag?) He promises to post pictures as a consolation prize. I read the next diary:

> Orpheus Online
> New York
>
> things got busy at constellation last night so i offered to help out. i served people vangoghs and directed them to the scopes. it was rewarding work although i decided to donate all $20 of my tips to durgha's outside labor fund. (she spends too much time roof gardening.) touching dirt is good for the soul, she tells me. she will (stubbornly) use the money for more purple geraniums. i use too many ((())).(good night)
>
> (orpheus)

He's always dropping names of places he's been to—movie theaters and nightclubs, even local Laundromats. But this feels like a particularly tantalizing clue about his life, so I put it in a search engine:

Orpheus + constellation

and I am rewarded instantly, directed to a cyberslutgirl's website. She has pix of herself in her slashed-up resewn outfits and teased-up hair with short diaries about her club experiences. One of them reads:

Went to constellation, the new star-viewing rooftop drink spot owned by orpheus and his honey bun, durgha. Drop $20 and you look at the stars thru giant telescopes, mingle with the divine, and get drinks called vangoes and Gallileos. They sure sent ME to the moon, honey. It IS the WORD. Livingston at the corner of east Second, right near the Green Kitty Cafe!!!!

His place! No matter that it is way past midnight and I am tracking down some nerd dude. I know I am going to Constellation and I've got that psychic quiet *click* sensation that he will be there when I go. I look for other mentions of Constellation on the Web, and I'm happy to see there aren't too many. The place has been around for six months already and is not that popular. Cool. Maybe I'll be able to talk to him there. Of course, he doesn't go there all the time. I find a tiny review in a food mag saying they serve lunch.

I can just imagine the place on a weekend night—tons of people packed in; maybe Orpheus wouldn't even show. But maybe he'd be there on a Sunday afternoon, like at four o'clock, too late for lunch and too early for dinner. I just know that's the time to go. Next Sunday, four o'clock. I go up to my room where I can use the phone without Ma waking. Zack gives me a joyful chirped greeting—like it's been years—and settles on my head. I call Information and Constellation is listed! I dial the digits and some girl answers—maybe it's the famous Durgha.

"Are you open at four o'clock on Sunday?" I say.

"Yes," she says, sounding totally pissed.

"Do you need reservations?"

"No, it's usually quiet then, you'll be fine." She actually hangs up.

I hang up and the phone rings immediately. My heart's in my throat, as if it were Orpheus. Then my Moon radar instantly snaps back into place and I grab the phone before it gets me killed.

"Hi," I say. I'm looking at the screen with all the Constellation info and I see it's two A.M. and I've been online for a while and for a second I feel like an insane girl. "I found this place that he owns and it's called Constellation—"

"Yeah I heard of that—" She sounds wary.

"And I want to go there with you next Sunday, I mean just to go in, and I just have this idea that—well, Moon, I feel pretty sure that we'll see him there."

"Yeah, and?"

"I don't know, and hang out."

"Just hang out with Orpheus?"

"Okay, it does sound stupid now, but want to?"

"Anooshka Star, are you all right, girl? I mean seriously, are you?"

I don't answer immediately. Maybe I am whacked. "Nah, my sis, I'm fine, I'm great. So let's go there, okay? Can I stay at your place next week?" I lower my voice. "I gotta get away from—you know."

"Our dear mamacita," she says. And then in a pseudo-wounded tone: "Didn't I tell you not to bring that painful subject up? And here you are again, rubbing it in my face that she loves you so much, you have to leave her smothering love—"

Eventually she says yeah. Elation dances through me. Then I'm up half the night, like I'm on speed, on my back in the dark, Orpheus in my earphones, seeing pictures in my mind, until Zack walks his hollow dinosaur claws right onto my face.

09. Chow Chow

Go dog go / go go go / go dog go dog go dog go

—from "Dog Cheer," © ORPHEUS XTIIMUSIC

Meet Taj. Shepherd, chow chow, bear. I like the velvet black underside of his chin and the black freckles on his tongue and his amber-eyed wolf gaze. Also, he makes an ecstatic commotion when I return from anywhere. Otherwise, I am not a big fan. I have been forced to walk him eight times since she brought him home two days ago. I have a count going, drawing checkmarks on my hand.

He lunges and pulls at the leash, and if I take him off the leash by the river he runs away like a coyote and plays Catch Me If You Can. On the way back from the walks, he nips at my ankles and tries to herd me like a sheep.

The first two hours she had him, Ma spent all her time on the computer finding the perfect name for him. She looked up rivers in Italy, Sioux prayers, Japanese colors, Hindu gods. And guess who was watching the puppy while this obsessive name search was going on?

At least she hired a guy to fence in the front yard with

chicken wire. But if you leave him out there for more than five minutes, he clops up onto the porch and scratches at the door with such power he has peeled the paint off. If you don't let the old bear in immediately, he smashes his paw against the front window. He already clawed through the screen and now we have to keep the window shut and the house is boiling.

Also, Zack does not like him. He wants to like him. He flies downstairs and sings to him, from a safe distance, perched on top of the fridge. Zack hasn't sat with us at the table once since Taj came.

This is Ma in the morning with him: "You're a chow chow, you know that?" On the floor with him in the kitchen, ruffling his fur, grabbing him onto her lap: "You're a chow, chow, chow, yes you are!"

He gazes at her with those googly, soft puppy eyes and then she screams at me to please take him for a walk.

Bear dog

10. My Timing Sucks

Why did you come by when I was feeling so happy?

—from "I Saw Jimi Hendrix in the Gym,"
© ORPHEUS XTIIMUSIC with Solaris Mudd (U.K. version)

Friday night. Less than two days to convince her to let me catch that Sunday morning bus. I work on her in my spare time, but no sign of her relenting. Have to tolerate her presence when she appears in my doorway.

"You just went to the city." She's a tiny person and yet she manages to loom. "It's forty-five dollars for a bus ticket to the city."

"That's why I have a job, Ma." And how I adore working those tables at the Zen Addict!

"Well, I don't have a job." (She throws in at least one random revelation per fight.)

"Right, well, you're on SSI." (Which proves you're insane, I don't add.) "And when I'm older, I'll be rich and successful and buy you a house on the Italian Riviera." (This usually pacifies her.)

"I don't like the idea of you roaming the city alone."

"I'll be with Moon."

"I'm just scared," she says.

Yeah, you always are. That's why you haven't left this town in twenty years. That's why you're on medication. That's why you make me feel like I'm the night nurse on Ward D. But your fear has nothing to do with me.

She looks past the whole surrealistic village on my windowsill, three years' worth of photos and collage set up in a perfect 3-D world. I don't want her probing into it with her eyes. Her gaze rests on the grinning photo of my father, the only one I have.

"And I don't see why you still have that up," she says in her whispery little hoarse voice that sometimes is too much like Moon's.

PA IS THE BEST!

I was ten when I visited him in California for the last time before he moved to India. He calls once or twice a year now, on my birthday and either Father's Day or his birthday and sometimes Christmas.

"Hi baby! Hi Nooshka Loushka! Newy Louey! How are you, honey? Did you get my letter? Are you doing good in school? I got a new baby rabbit today. I'm driving a blue truck these days. The weather here is beautiful."

He's just as crazy as she is, but I hardly know him so

he seems less. I've never hated him. He's just a blank place in my chest whenever someone says "dad." Red hair, red face, blond eyebrows, squinty blue eyes, tall as a mountain, wearing shirts rolled up at the sleeve. Always smiling, smoking cigarettes, getting new pets and getting rid of them all the time like a profession.

But I do remember the photographs he took of people on the edge; I thought they were a little scary but cool. He taught me that it was worth it to capture pieces of the world. And I remember him shaking his head in terse little agreeing shakes when the therapist said Ma was making me nuts. I shook my head yes, too.

Why do I have the damn picture up? Maybe just to annoy her. But I don't say this.

"Maybe you can go," she concedes.

I should leave it at that, but I don't want to deal with her maddening vagueness. I want to go in two days and I want it all sealed up.

"When will you know?"

"Anooshka, just give me a break. It's almost midnight. I've had a hard day, and if you push me I'm going to have to just say no."

Sometimes I want to take her little head and bash it against the wall.

"Okay, Ma," I say, swallowing the rage.

Without warning, Ma's back again, an hour later, grinning at me with a bubblegum pink mouth that makes her look like a drag queen. "What do you think?" she shouts above the music. She's wearing a new spandex workout getup.

I lower the volume. "About what?" It feels as if this procedure will go on all night.

"This whole new look—I think Frank likes this sort of thing—I just get the feeling that he's into pink lipstick, the curvy look, you know—"

"It's great. You look gorgeous."

It's been years since I tried to talk her out of her obsessions. I used to plead with her. You're good enough the way you are, Ma. You're beautiful, perfect. Don't try to make your boobs look smaller for the architect who likes flat-chested ballet dancers. Don't dye your hair black for the guy you met online who's hot for Italian women. Don't take yoga, learn to snowboard, talk less, laugh more, be bitchier, practice silence—don't let anyone make you crazier than you are. But she was never happy unless she had put a collar around her neck and handed her leash to some guy.

When it came to men, she and Moon were on opposite sides—one holding the hoop and one jumping through.

"Is the gym open at one A.M. or something?"

"Just trying on stuff for—tomorrow," she says, smiling

at herself, checking out her ass in my mirror. It's so gross to think of your mother as having an ass. But there's a cheery mood between us, and it seems like the right time, so I jump right in:

"So can I go, Ma? I need to know."

She gives me a cold look. "God, I fall for flattery every time. You will just have to wait until tomorrow!"

My timing sucks, but I wasn't flattering her; I meant it. Now I'm too pissed to straighten it out. Who invented this system of mothers and teenagers living together?

11. Psycho Ma

They can kill you / but they can't get you / in a bad mood

—from "Chain Reaction," © ORPHEUS XTIIMUSIC

Sunday, bright and early, wrapped in a sense of doom.
If Ma does not let me go to the city today, I'll go anyway.

They say you should appreciate what you have, and I try.

Sometimes when I'm eating I see children, sick from hunger. If you love your food, can you eat for them? Can you run for the ones who can't walk? An idea hangs ahead of me, huge and unknowable as the sun: someday I will do something to alleviate suffering.

Ma would say, why don't you start by alleviating *my* suffering and change your attitude? (Or go play with Taj, who's whimpering in the front yard.) And in a way, she's right. But no matter how good I have it compared to tons of other people, I can't help the feeling I get of being trapped.

Alone with Ma, in this small town, where it's winter eight months a year and rains most of the summer, with nowhere to go but the woods or the mall. A big cage, with a cleverly simulated habitat, but it still has bars.

It's not too late to catch the one-thirty bus, if only Ma would say yes. Because, who am I kidding, I don't have the guts to break out.

Overnight, the river's turned a murky reddish brown and is rushing with triple force. The rain falls silently, fine as mist. I press my face against the screen. The air is warm and slushy, gray and tropical. Two crazy little ducks float by, bobbing smoothly on the river, moving in unison like mini-kayakers. I don't know why, but there's something hilarious about ducks on the river in the rain. Maybe their blank expressions.

Still in my red monkey pj's. A few moments to be myself, with Ma safely at the gym again. Found out that this Frank character works out in the mornings. Big surprise.

Maybe I should do a few sit-ups? Nah.

I flick on the Orpheus CD, climb up to my bed as the first rumble of drums begins, click on my laptop.

Orpheus Online
New York
joyride

imagine if a thousand years from now everyone forgot everything about christmas except for the fact that Santa flew through the air in a sleigh pulled by reindeer. they forget about Jesus, the presents, the candy canes, the tree. all that survives is the ride in the sky.

i guess this is bragging, but orphism was the main religion in ancient greece, thousands of years ago.

the myth of orpheus and eurydice was just a tiny part of the religion, but their wild story is the only part of the religion that everyone remembers. probably because they were even cooler than romeo and juliet.

orpheus

Oh, goody—history and myths! Just those words make my mind go dead. But something in his tone hooks me.

Orpheus Online
New York
the darn snake ruined everything

orpheus and eurydice are crazy in love. she is bitten by a snake and falls down to the underworld of death. he goes down after her and sings a begging song to the unearthly guardians of that world. his lute and his words make hearts melt, wild animals calm and cold people cry.

his song is so compelling, they let him lead eurydice up into the aboveworld. the only catch is, he is not allowed to look back at her until they are safely up. he takes her hand and they begin their journey. . . .

orpheus

I can guess where we're heading, but I don't get confirmation, because Ma's car drives up. Feet up the stairs. Barely knocking at my door before she's in. Her presence altering the molecular structure of my room.

She's all happy, with an inextinguishable smile. Even though I'm irritated by her, I can't help noticing that her hair looks perfect, little pieces sticking out in just the right way, a skinny braid with a baby barrette near the front. Hey—

"That's my daisy barrette," I say.

Her face darkens. "That's all you have to say? Not even good morning? Not hello—"

"I said hello." I click on the exit window. Do not want Orpheus's site to be tainted by her looking at it, her questions, her anything.

"You're online, aren't you?" she says. "You know, Anooshka, you've been home all morning and you didn't even clean the kitchen. You have one job to do on the weekends, for not even an hour, and you don't even do it.

You've been online all this time, haven't you?"

She says "online" as if it is some kind of pornographic club.

"I'm researching a project for social studies," I tell her.

"What are you studying?" She edges over, standing on her toes, craning to see the screen, which is just showing my desktop.

I cannot keep the annoyance out of my voice. "Greek myths, Ma, okay?"

"Greek mythology!" She is thrilled.

"Ma, what are you doing?" I say. She's actually on my ladder, starting to climb. She freezes.

"I studied myths with Joseph Campbell, you know that, so I don't see why you don't—"

"Ma—can I please have some privacy?" I want to scoop up my laptop and jump off the side of the bed.

"Fine!" Ma backs down with a little snarl on her face. "Damn you, Anooshka! I was in such a good mood. I wanted to tell you about my morning and then I come home and you ruined my mood, just ruined it!"

Sometimes I stay quiet and let her storms pass. This time it just comes out of me: "Well, I was in a good mood, too. Maybe you're ruining my mood!"

"Just shut up," she says. "You know—" Her voice breaks and I almost feel sorry for her. She uses her super-quiet killer voice. "I just realized that it's summer.

Summer! You don't have social studies in the *summer!* You are such a smartass these days, I can't even deal with you." She comes toward my bed as if to be menacing, but it's not possible to feel threatened by someone that small. She backs up and then yanks the plastic barrette out of her hair and throws it at me. I have to stop myself from laughing.

"Schizoid," I say under my breath.

Her green eyes grow cold. "What did you say?"

"Nothing, Ma, I said nothing."

"Just stay in your room until you're ready to apologize to me!"

She slams out of my room as I say: "Fine—sorry!"

The room feels smaller after she leaves, as if my frustration has taken up all the airspace. Fall back on the bed, stare at the ceiling. Tears brewing and I tell them to leave. This always happens after we fight. I don't even know why I'm sad or even if I'm sad. Is there such a thing as tears of frustration? Tears of guilt? I ruined her good mood. And the pathetic way she threw that barrette—it makes my heart fold up like a plastic fortune fish. Zack looks deeply at me, our hearts connected, and then he hops off my finger onto my face, walking across it as if I am inanimate.

THE BAD VIBES ARE SUFFOCATING.

I stand at the window with Zack on my shoulder. The rain's making circles in the river and I open the window to breathe in the sizzly smell. A wild bird chirps on a willow branch just a few inches from my face. Zack chirps back, and I can feel the tight energy in his body and that pang in the heart from his attempt to connect with the outside world.

The man

The wild bird is brown and has a dumb, harsh look in its eyes. Its head moves like a puppet head—left, right, and then it flies off into the gray sky.

Zack made his second escape when he was about five years old. We'd been letting him fly loose in the house for years, since his first escape.

It was a summer day and the door was open and we watched him zoom and dip across the meadow. It was an exhilarating moment, and I could only think how happy he would be playing with the other birds. He was gone for two days. Every day we would look for him at the edge of the woods, calling him and holding his cage. One day he just flew down. He scrambled into the cage and sidled next to his fake plastic green bird and talked to it for an hour straight, all happy and excited. He ate like a starved man and slept for twenty-four hours. Then he was normal and cheerful again.

"You little Zackie," I tell him. I make the chirping noise with my lips and then the clicking noise with my tongue, and he does it back to me and I do it back to him. We have this little bird convo for a minute, and then he suddenly takes off flying, leaving a tiny piece of bird poop on my shoulder.

"Thanks so much, Zack," I say, flicking it off.

Ma sticks her head in. "Okay, Nooshka, honey, you can go." She looks quite pleased with herself.

I don't even ask why or what changed her mind. Grab

her in a hug. Start throwing things in a bag. Pick up the phone to call Moon. Sift birdseed into Zack's tray. Look out the window at the guy honking and see the reason Ma relented. She's got a date with Gym Guy. God bless him.

"Just call me as soon as you get to Moon's apartment!" she yells, bouncing out of the house.

12. Constellation

Shock us Mrs. Ska Rocket / with your leaf star and harp

—from "Hailbopper QT," © ORPHEUS XTIIMUSIC

I've got the door of the cab open, as if that will help. She's out there spinning in the late-afternoon sunshine, her hair all side-lit and glowing burgundy, giving one more laughing, nuzzling, nose-rubbing kiss to Marley. He's MTV meets caveman in his parchment-colored rags. The odd, thickly beaded leather and metal strands at his wrists and neck look painful and magical, like a martyr's jewels, but they won't help him, his beautiful sad mouth won't help, the tattooed snake around his neck will not help, the tiny tattooed stars by his left eye will not help. Nothing will keep my sister from speeding off with me. Marley stands there solid and tragic, tall and sculpted, elaborately brooding. He tugs at her, for one last hopeless embrace. I'm glad to be leaving; I just spent two hours walking all over the city with these love doves. They stopped at every red light to kiss and missed every other green light while I trotted around after them and tried to look as happily self-contained as somebody's pet lab.

I stick my head out. "Jesus, Moon! You're gonna hook up in a few hours—what is the big deal?"

Marley's giving her the drowning look and she is tormenting him with her lightness. I have seen this so many times with so many guys. It's still mesmerizing, but it's almost four and that is the time *we have to be there*!

The cab's already costing us, and we haven't left the curb. The driver sees me checking the meter and gives me a juicy wink.

"Is your sister?"

"Hey, how'd you know?"

He shrugs. "She acts like sister."

Moon finally slides into the car, all smelling like Marley. Why do her boys always smell so good, like leather jackets and airport bars? She is flushed with happiness. The beginning is always the good time, when she has all of their attention and when they briefly have hers. In three weeks she'll be over him.

"Don't you love him?" she asks as we lurch off, galumphing over potholes, the driver calmly cursing, swerving and leaning on his horn.

"Yeah, he's great," I say. I don't even know the dude. He seems like his predecessors, but I would not tell her this. Every new boy is Moon's idol until he becomes irritating.

Showing up late, flirting with other girls, wearing white socks, having a too-round forehead—these are all fatal crimes. Not that she's shallow. The real Moon does not care about skin, height, socks, time. Her soul is a bowl of coconut curry stew. She just has a few fears to overcome. A few things that make love impossible for her so far. When she was my age, she went out with guys named Killer and Snake who treated her like killers and snakes, and she was obsessed with them. Not only did she fail to notice their lies and pot addictions and white socklike habits, she forgave them everything!

In the middle of her very last major drama queen heartbreak, the cycle was broken when, out of nowhere, a truly nice boy met her in the park and fell in love with her. From then on she was like an enchanted creature, attracting the cute boys and tossing them away when they got too close.

"So this is something new you've got us into." She settles back into the seat, happily leaning on me. "This manic moment," she croons. I punch her shoulder, even though I know she could be talking about either of us, the way we dive without caution.

Next thing, the taxi lets us off on First Avenue and we're looking for the place. The whole neighborhood has a sleepy, closed-down feeling, with narrow streets and lots of dark-faced thrift stores, bakeries, and coffee shops. We both spot the small guy with a baseball cap and snaky dark hair as he comes out of a little place across the street, right on the corner of Second Avenue and Livingston.

Moon looks at me in astonishment. "This is way too easy. Is it—?"

"I don't know—let's follow him!" The guy ducks into a newspaper store and we're on him like white on rice.

"It could be him," Moon says. "Maybe he needs a pack of cigs or—"

"He doesn't smoke."

She looks at me. "Check you out! I forgot—you know all the details."

The guy disappears in the back. The man behind the tall counter is scowling down at us beneath bushy brows. My heart is pounding. The place is chilled and smells like old lettuce and overheated coffee. I have a swelling fondness for the place because it is Orpheus's newspaper store and Orpheus himself is in this store. I stall for time, pretending to consider various candies, and then reach in my pocket for a buck for a pack of bubblegum. Mr. Hair soon reemerges, pushing a delivery cart loaded with a few boxes. He's probably fifty years old.

Moon and I exchange a look, and we're back onto the street. And then I really do see him, unmistakably him, right across the street, standing outside this towering faceless building, the tallest building on the block. I see the flash of his glasses in the sunshine. He's wearing jeans and sneakers and a black T-shirt with something on the front. I grip Moon's arm and she sees him too. I almost run straight across the street, although everything inside me is warning: be calm, be cool, chill, chill. Then he slips inside the building.

As soon as we step into the building, the neighborhood feeling is gone. The interior is all gray with a razor-thin strip of violet neon running along the wall where it meets the seam of the high ceiling. Our feet sink into thick, sound-absorbing carpet. It feels like an otherworldly library or Gucci showroom. Where's the single pairs of two-thousand-dollar shoes embalmed in glass cylinders? People in uniform sit behind a curved, raised embankment that looks like it's carved out of one piece of polished granite. A velvet rope blocks us from a wall of elevators. Orpheus is probably on his way up.

We sign in and tell them our destination is Constellation. They are cool as scientists. They give us guest passes, which we attach to our clothes with clips.

In the elevator ZZ Moon is all excited and squirmy, in spite of herself—and I'm so glad.

"Aren't you freaking?" she says. "Why are you so calm? You're going to see him! Your psychic powers are totally working!"

We hit the sixteenth floor and my ears pop. Twenty more floors to go. "I was picturing this place as a cute little sidewalk cafe."

"No, you nut," she says. "I told you, it's on the roof. It's all about telescopes and stars. Constellation, get it?"

Sometimes I miss the obvious. Moon's on her cell with Ma. "Yeah, we just got to my place." She passes me the phone, I get off real quick, lova ya, mwah, etc.

The door of the elevator opens and things get immediately cool.

The elevator goes black, a rumbling chord of Orpheus's keyboard fills the space, and I do mean space. It's as if we are already inside a planetarium, staring out into pure blackness with pinpricks of stars on the wall and ceiling. A pleasant female voice booms out: "Please do not exit the elevator. Wait for the lights."

A steady, booming drumbeat kicks in. The lights fly on and we step blinking out of the elevator into a long, narrow hallway pulsing with Orpheus music, a silver painted arrow leading to a shiny, thick, round chrome door.

The interior's got the subdued feeling of an airport cocktail lounge. It's all gray and modern and metal and dimly lit in spite of a long, high bank of windows along the side wall. There is the sense of being on a slow-moving futuristic battleship. It's not a large room, but not cozy either.

A few Eurohipster types sit at the tiny tables bolted into the floor. A tall girl, skinny as a twelve year old, with bright red baby dreads, gives us a quick look from behind the bar and decides to ignore us. I think I've seen her picture on the Orpheus site. I've been operating on this adrenal pull for days, propelled by that physical yearning to experience the connection again. Suddenly I'm flooded with doubt: maybe he won't want to see me. Maybe he's off in some back room. We head for the ornately carved gothic doors leading to an outside area.

Sudden quiet. A hot wind on the roof. Scattered benches. Tropical trees in pots. Plants everywhere. Hundreds of purple flowers in pots. A dozen telescopes mounted to the five-foot wall at the roof's edge. Maybe Orpheus, over there by the little cafe-style tables.

"Hey, there's your sidewalk cafe," Moon says.

"Yeah." The sky's pale blue, cloudless. The air is mild. That is definitely Orpheus. He's sitting with an older guy who has a stack of papers out on the table. Time slows. I feel like a star. Maybe this place is magic and that walk through the tunnel just strips you of all your problems and leaves you clean and amazing and shiny.

We walk right past Orpheus and put our things on a polished silver table near him. There's only five other people here, no one acting all psyched and insane about Orpheus.

We look at the menus. I sneak a look at Orpheus. He's looking right at me, smiling, recognition in his eyes. Moon gives me a worried look as if she doesn't want me to get my hopes up. How could this be so easy, like he summoned me without a phone. I've always heard that when souls are really connected, it comes easy—it's just the co-dependent, twisted relationships that go through all the torment.

The Baby Red Dread Girl comes into the area and scoots right in beside Orpheus. She's got to be that Durgha he's always talking about. Leans on his shoulder. My heart sinks. Knock that off, I tell myself. You didn't even kiss him. He can have a girlfriend. No he can't.

A waitress comes over to their table. I can't hear him ordering, his voice low and mumbly. But I hear the red dread girl, her voice loud and annoying:

"And I'll have a carrot juice," she says. "I've been grazing all day."

I haven't grazed at all and I'm starving. The only thing I had during the love dove tour of the city was a pretzel with mustard from a street vendor.

"Man, this stuff is pricey," whispers ZZ Moon.

The only items on the menu we can afford are the desserts. They all sound beautiful and delicate, and we decide on chocolate flan and wild strawberries in pomegranate creme, and jasmine flower tea ice cream. Each fourteen dollars.

The waitress takes our order and my eyes flick over to Orpheus again and there's that sweet smile.

I have no choice. "Can I talk to you?" I ask him. My right shin is instantly, painfully kicked. I give the kicker a sharp look. I didn't plan on asking him.

His smile vanishes. Baby Red Dread Girl actually turns her back to me. "In a little while," he says, a little shyly. "When I'm through eating," he says.

"Great, thanks."

Moon's eyes are huge. "What are you doing?" she whispers. "You're insane." But I feel powerful. I'm here, he's going to talk to me, it's all working out. "Come on," I say. "Let's go look at the view." I swagger off like a cowboy.

Our waitress is clearing away our spotless plates. Orpheus is still lingering over his food. Baby Red Dread is so clingy with him, leaning on him, head on his shoulder, giving him quick hugs. He doesn't swat her away, but he doesn't return the affection either. I get this older brother vibe. She jumps up now and scoots over to a deep planter, reaching her hand in to feel the dirt.

"It is so dry," she announces. "It gets so dry up on the roof, Orph, you have no idea. All I do is water."

In a flash I imagine being her, owning this place with Orpheus and already taking it for granted. The place as familiar as your own bathroom. Orpheus as familiar as a cousin. The watering chores tedious. Orpheus always leaving for some glamorous tour . . .

I wonder if she's in love with him or he with her. Nah, it's gotta be that sib thing. She trots back into the building. Orpheus is talking to the older guy in his low voice. He signs a few papers. The guy slides them into a black briefcase. "So I'll see you there," he says.

"Right," says Orpheus. They stand. They give each other a quick manly embrace. The guy goes off past our table, flashing us a little peace sign as he passes.

Except for three motherly looking women at a table and a couple gazing out at the roof's edge, we are alone with Orpheus. Weird, he doesn't have bodyguards.

He's coming toward us. Until this second I've been feeling light and big, like a balloon. My heart has turned into a weight, slamming against my rib cage. ZZ Moon's letting out that whispery, strangled squeal she gets when she's excited but trying to keep it down, like when you're hiding behind someone's door at a surprise party.

"Hi," he says, giving me a steady gaze and that hopeful smile.

I shoot my hand out and he ignores it, giving me a quick, light embrace and a kiss on the cheek. Before I can feel too special, he does the same to Moon. I could be imagining it, but I swear she shoots him a stern, don't you mess with my sister look. He doesn't seem to notice.

He looks at me expectantly. Quick. I have to say something. I asked him if I could talk to him—not if he could talk to me. Now *talk*, girl. All those hours reading his diary and steeped in his music, it's hard to shake the conviction that I intimately know him, correction, that we intimately *know each other*.

But now, looking into his gentle face, those complicated eyes, I realize he does not know me at all and has no idea that I know him. I am just any fan at the moment, unable to speak, acting like I expect him to perform. God. I'm like those girls on his website. I should be home kissing his CD cover. Quick, I order myself to think something, quick—do something—sing—touch him—dance—hurry—

I sit there stupidly smiling.

"I hope you enjoyed the food," he says. "I'm actually getting ready to go on tour. Got a lot of ends to tie up. I have a concert tonight, and we're starting a little tour tomorrow."

"Wow," I say. Moon notes my eloquence with a pitying look.

"My sister," she says quickly, totally winging it. "She wants to know—" She freezes, looks at me to fill in the blanks.

"Yeah, I want to know—"

He cocks his head slightly, the smile spreading. "Yes?"

"Those telescopes—can we use them in the daytime?" Oh*God*ohGodohGod, idiot!!!!!!!!!!

"Yes, good question, yes, you can. Come on, I have a little time—" He checks his watch. "A few minutes, anyway. I'll show you."

I'm watching him, feeling his warmth as he stands near me. He swings the scopes around here and there, and we catch a nude couple on their roof garden doing some sort of martial arts routine. Then there's a woman with a head wrap leaning out her window with her face tilted to the sky. A guy on the sidewalk, three blocks over, walking five dogs. We take turns swinging and sharing the views.

"It's like a daytime constellation," I say.

Orpheus gives me an odd look.

"Of people," I say quickly, reddening. "Like everyone's in their own specific orbit, but they all fit together in some way that we haven't figured out yet."

The three of us stand there, blinking and breathing in the warm air.

"I always think that," Orpheus says. "That exact thing." He's looking at me with new awareness.

Moon hesitates, then drifts to the other side of the roof, to give us some space. "You're so complex," he says, low. "You're like oxygen, you know?" The intimate feeling comes up so thick it seems like a tangible entity. He stands so close I can feel his breathing. Moon's not looking, there's no one else on the roof—he could kiss me now, I would let him—

Then he looks at his watch and says he has to go. Invisible shields seem to drop over his eyes. He's so polite he actually thanks *us*, and then he's walking briskly off.

"Have a great tour," I shout to his back. He holds up his arm without turning around.

I feel empty. We start to leave. . . .

"Wait," says Orpheus. Enigmatic smile, head tilted. "I've got a few passes, I mean, if you guys want them—"

He is so casual, reaching in his jeans pocket, handing the passes to us like they're nothing. Thanks, we say, matching his tone, even though our bodies are rising lightly off the ground.

13. Orpheus

His stuff

*We all dream / isn't that the point / we all dream /
there is no point / everything's round*

—from "Kamina Royale," © ORPHEUS XTIIMUSIC
with Mitake Ganesh

We're shoved in tight, pushed up against the edge of the stage. People are sway-dancing, mouthing the words, stinking of pot and sweat. Intense music: tribal, exotic, a loud harmony of triple drumming, sudden horns, gospel singers. A wheeze of accordion, resounding organ chords, samples of crackly whorehouse jazz and classical viola, three girls in wheelchairs moving their arms in ballet gestures.

I'm close enough to see his hair—dark, wet strands swept into his face. There's fiery joy in his eyes, a scar next to his temple. I'm thinking, I met him. I know him. He asked me here. The personal connection beats in me like a rhythmic undertone to the music.

Sparks catch in the gems glued to his skin. He's charged with charisma, like some kind of god up there. He knows he owns us.

Now the three-ring troupe moves back in the shadows and Orpheus pulls up a stool under a single violet light, lifting a simple guitar of polished wood off a stand. His hand moves slowly, sliding up and down the guitar neck, each chord shimmering in the air. He keeps his face mostly down but when he looks up, his dark sea eyes drift across the crowd and I'm surfing on a wave of ecstatic fear.

"I think he's looking at me," Moon says in my ear, and I wonder how many people are having that fantasy. And then I swear his eyes abruptly find mine and he breaks into the soft smile of recognition.

Backstage turns out to be a long line in a shabby parking lot behind the concert building. We're by the West Side docks and a warm, garbagey breeze comes off the river. A pudgy guard with sunglasses blocks the top of the stairs, opening the door for select people. I've been watching carefully—apparently the people with laminated passes breeze in while the ones clutching stars are kept waiting.

I'm jangling with nervous energy, and Moon, who's usually calm, is anything but.

"I can't believe we're here!" she says, dancing in place like a hyperactive boxer, giving me strangling hugs around the neck.

"If you hadn't called Ma this morning—" She'd assured Ma she'd take excellent care of me and she promised to come visit next weekend. She hasn't been home in months and I know she'll find some excuse not to come, but Ma bought it.

The Orpheus music runs in my head and my ears are still ringing. Instead of feeling unreal, the night feels superreal to me, a heightened sense of camaraderie as well as competition in the air—like we're all in this together, but only some of us are going to win.

There's a massive silver tour bus parked at the far side

of the lot. And everyone keeps wondering if *he's* in it.

"He's definitely watching us," says a girl, breaking into an exaggerated dance and butt wiggle for whoever's behind the smoked glass windows. She's cute but she smells like the devil. I take a few steps back.

"Don't waste your moves, girl," says her rooster-haired boyfriend. "He's not in there. He's in a backstage john, shooting up."

"Orpheus doesn't do drugs," Moon chimes in. She says it with such pleasant authority in her vibrating husk of a voice.

"Dude, she's right," says Stinko Girl.

"Yeah, maybe," admits Rooster Boy. "Yeah, he's weird like that, huh? He's like afraid to drink coffee. I definitely heard that somewhere."

They light up clove cigs, and we move away from the sweet smoke clouds.

Z's latest creation is a choker of pale pink stones with complicated knotted threads between them and tiny silver bells. I lift it off her neck and catch a whiff of her scent. She smells so good she cancels out the other girl. "This one's amazing," I tell her, touching the delicate necklace.

"I'll make one for you." She gets that dreamy look, already planning. "Just tell me the colors you want."

Lately I haven't been into jewelry—just texture, mixing fragile with industrial. Tonight I almost wore one of

Moon's creations—this raggedly stitched dress made from a cut-up army shirt and a bright tangerine tank. It made my skin look so white. Moon's skin gets golden and bronzed and mine burns. I decided to go with the paleness and be simple: black T-shirt and jeans and flat black sneakers.

"Look what I'm wearing," I say. "It's so goth. Or uninspired eighties."

She studies me. "You look more like a Bohemian waif."

"But it's boring, right?"

"Girl, I keep telling you, when you're gorgeous, your beauty is emphasized by simple clothes."

"Gorgeous, right."

"Look at you! With those cheekbones and those big eyes. Your incredible smile. Now shut up, you vain thing."

"But Mickey gave me the pass." A woman in her thirties hands the guard her star. "It's a VIP pass." She looks like she stepped out of an all-purple 1969 stage set—dressed in violet, from her cowboy boots to her floppy vintage hat.

The guard examines the star, pretending to think it over. "This thing isn't worth jack," he says. "But if you go back down there and wait patiently, like everybody else, I might let you in later." He waves his hand dismissively.

Ms. Purple stands firm. By now we're all hooked, like she's the champion of our cause. "Call Mickey up on your cell," she says. "Just call him and he'll tell you."

The guard's pissed now. "You need to get lost," he says. "I mean now, before I really call someone." He punctuates every word with a jab of his cell. "Get the hell to the end of the line!"

She's pissed but complies.

"What about us?" I ask Moon. "Do you think we'll get in?" She's been to a few concerts and even went backstage once when her ex-boyfriend was a roadie for Second Skin.

"Definitely," says Moon, her eyes shiny as Chinese firecrackers. "I can feel it."

We're out there for a while, beginning to lose hope, when a guy comes off the silver bus.

"Hey Joey!" The woman in the floppy hat scoots out from the end of the line. Joey, a guy in a visor with a curly beard, hears her out, nodding, nodding as she tells how the guard wouldn't let her backstage to see the flute player.

"Okay, she's good," he tells the guard, and the woman has the grace to throw us an apologetic shrug before striding up the stairs and through the open door.

I'm so absorbed by this drama that I jerk back when Joey taps me on the shoulder. "Hey, how you doin'?" he says, with the kind of smile you use for old friends. I can feel Moon tense up, ready to protect me. Back off, I tell her silently. Maybe the guy will let us backstage at last. "Come here a sec, would you?" He pulls me a little away from the line. Moon tails.

"Michael wants to see you." He jerks his head in the direction of the bus.

"Who?"

Moon breathes in sharply. "Orpheus. His real name." My insides lurch.

"He's on the bus," says Joey. "If you feel like hanging out."

"Can my sister come?"

He checks Moon out, and suddenly I see her as he must—the real star, everything about her intriguing and radiant. He hesitates, and for a second I just know he's realizing the mistake he made: Orpheus wants her, not me.

Then:

"Look, I'd like to say yes," he tells Moon. "But he asked specifically for this one." He quickly softens the ominous sound of that. "He's a good guy, don't worry."

Moon blinks away her disappointment and becomes mother hen. "You're not going anywhere in that bus, are you?" She looks up at the dark windows as if they'll turn transparent. "When will she be out? Who else is on there?" I haven't even said I want to go—everyone just assumes it's a given. I'm afraid to speak and ruin things.

"Relax, the bus isn't moving." The reassuring big brother. "We're not taking off until tomorrow. Let them chat for a while and then you can hook up with us for the after-party. Hey, if it makes you feel better, I'll keep an eye on her."

"Moon—," I start. Our eyes lock and she knows she doesn't have a choice.

"Okay, go," she says, forcing a smile. She leans in close. "Just, Anooshka—well, you know. You know." Without saying a word, she's telling me to remember everything she ever taught me, like she's sending me off on a trip.

"You can go backstage—," offers Joey, ready to wave her past the guard.

"That's okay," says Moon. "I'm gonna stay here."

Joey settles me in a comfy seat facing another seat with a table in between, more like a living room arrangement than a bus. The table's messy with a crumpled takeout bag, stack of CDs, two half-drunk bottles of Corona. He disappears in the back, saying he's going to get Michael.

Music blasts through the bus, one guitar solo from the concert played and replayed. In between plays I hear bursts of laughter, people discussing it, someone pointing out a flaw. In a strange way it reminds me of when Moon and I were little and accused of some wrongdoing and my father used to whip out his secret tapes of our conversations. Our viewpoints could never stand up under his scrutiny. We'd be saying no, I didn't eat that last piece of cake, she did it,

I swear, and he'd say listen to your voice tremble. Hear that? That part there! And finally we'd admit that it hadn't been the other sibling. He never got that mad in the end— it was more about ferreting out the error and assigning appropriate blame. Our punishment was hearing ourselves lie on tape.

I peer across the lot at the people in line. Moon's sitting with her back against the building, talking to some guy. I try to imagine what Orpheus saw when he saw me standing there.

While I'm sifting through the CDs—no one I've heard of—some guy from the back slides into the seat across from me. He's small and his hair's dripping wet and he's saying:

"Was I all right? How was I?" He looks like a thing newly broken out of its shell.

I'm on the brink of escape, and then—I recognize him.

"Yeah, you were amazing," I tell him. "You were incredible."

He's talking nonstop like he's on some drug, then stops every so often to look at me.

"I thought you were basic," he says. "But you're so complex." His words sound like lyrics, or maybe they just have a ring of significance because he's saying them. I memorize them instantly.

Are you my angel? he says. *You seem like one.*

107

And: *You're so perfect.*

No one ever said those things to me.

Then he goes back to talking about the show as if I'm a fellow musician. Did I like the part where all the drums stopped one by one until it was one stick, one drum, slowly beaten? What about when they switched to the minor chord in the middle of the Beauty song? Did I like the way they played "Remember That Night" with the picked-up tempo? Didn't I dig the syncopation in the—

"The girl don't know the meaning of syncopation," breaks in a guy across the aisle. While we've been talking, people have drifted up from the back and settled in around us. "Why don't you stop talking and buy her an ice cream?" The guy, an older bass player with pouchy eyes and a toothy grin, leans in close to us. He's got a cigarette lighter in his hand. "Mind if I do the honors?" he says to me, holding the lighter near the frayed cuffs of my jeans. I think of Moon outside—will she know it's me when she sees the flames?

Instead he just does this little trick—lights the threads and they burn off without the jeans catching fire. "This is JD," says Orpheus. "He's famous. JD, give her your autograph."

"I don't remember how to do that, but she can have this." He tosses me his lighter. "Just don't try that trick at home, boys and girls."

"Yeah, take mine, too," says Orpheus, producing a black three-dollar lighter from his pocket. "I hardly even smoke." Even though he's taking the lighter back from me now, to smoke a hit of something off a pipe. I don't take any, but I sip a lukewarm beer, which is making me feel a little sick. I keep looking at his face, trying to see the humble guy in the maze, trying to see the icon up onstage. The only thing that's the same is his eyes. When he talks, they dart around like he's wild. He's so distracted, at once so insecure and obsessed with his performance, he's hard to get a fix on. When he leans in to ask me if I'm his angel for the second time—*Seriously, are you an angel?*—it seems as if he might try to kiss me, but he doesn't and I'm relieved, I think.

I want to ask him if he remembers me from the maze and if he saw me when he was up onstage. But those are stupid things to ask a star, so I keep it a mystery for now.

There are certain things that come along that take precedence over all other events, like natural catastrophes, car accidents, and unexpected meetings with rock stars. These things suck you in entirely and leave no room for you to wonder how bored or worried other people might be while you are so completely engaged. I forget about Moon. My eyes are fixed on his face. I barely speak. At one point I ask:

"Is your real name Michael?"

"No one calls me that but Joey. We go back. Would you rather call me that?" This is his charm, so concerned and familiar.

Out of nowhere he gives my hand a squeeze. The squeeze goes directly into my stomach, and I don't know whether it's excitement or fear. He keeps holding my hand. I think of my hands as big, but they're small next to his. He has long fingers and large, rounded fingernails. I'm so dumb, staring at his hand. He gives another gentle squeeze. "You don't mind, do you? Is this okay?" I smile and look away; it's so embarrassing to be asked. "Aw, don't worry," he says. "Hey, you're a little scared of me, aren't you?" He gets up and scoots around, sitting next to me. My heart's a loud machine. He picks my hand up again, lacing his fingers in mine, raising it to his face suddenly to examine my fresh-drawn notes and designs. He starts reading the numbers out loud—"Oh, hey—you're that girl—from the beach, right?" He seems to look at me for the first time. "Whoa, twice in one week; must be fate."

So he didn't remember until now. Even though he was the one who gave us the passes.

"I'm going to give you some breathing room," he says, slipping back across from me. "And keep this." He presses his black lighter into my hand and closes my fingers over it. "In honor of our second meeting." He laughs, a warm, infectious laugh. "Sorry I was so rude. Sometimes things come over me."

"It's three times," I say, but he doesn't hear me.

"Come on, gotta go." Joey's been trying to hustle him out for a while.

"Just one more minute," Orpheus keeps telling him. "I'm having fun with—"

He leans in to me, puts his hand on mine, and it scares me. He looks into my eyes and says really low, so only I can hear: "Tell me your name one more time and I'll never forget it."

I tell him.

"Yeah, Anooshka is my new best friend, I'm happy now, don't you care?"

"They're waiting for you—"

We gaze out the windows—quite a crowd out there now.

"Ah, paparazzi," says Orpheus, looking a little pleased.

"My sister's out there." Even though I don't see her.

"Your sister?" I'm afraid he's going to say something lewd, but he's concerned instead, like a grandmother. "We've gotta do something about that. Joey—we've got to take better care of Anooshka's people."

The band's gathering their stuff, heading off the bus. Two cars pull up alongside it, engines idling. "Let's just grab her sister and get out of here—I don't want to deal with all those people."

"But they're your fans." I can't help it. "They've been waiting to see you. . . ." I clap my hand over my own big mouth, but he doesn't seem offended.

"You think so? Should I? Hey Joey, Anooshka thinks I should go say hi to the public." Again, that sense that we're in it together.

"Go for it." Joey looks at me like, good job. "PR never hurts."

More cars pull up by the bus, and Joey says it's now or never.

"Just stay near me," Orpheus tells me. "Don't get away."

But as we troop off the bus, we're swept apart. For a moment I feel so amazingly proud, coming off the bus with him and the whole band, cameras flashing in my face.

Moon's at my side, grabbing my hand. Joey hustles us into one of the cars. I'm jammed between Moon and a big woman, and in the crush, and in the dense excitement, I can hardly take a breath. The car speeds up like the night.

14. He Locks Us In

I don't want you to dance with me /
just go into a trance with me

—from "Muse," © ORPHEUS XTIIMUSIC

It's this ethereal hotel with bamboo floors and rock gardens, silent fountains in cool tones of slate and green. When you get high up, you can see out to the dark meadows of Central Park South. Once you're inside the party suite, there's not that much of a meditative vibe. Orpheus himself is the most Zen thing in the room.

The energy flows around him, of course, and he looks like he loves it, all kicked back on the low, overstuffed Japanese couch, happy as a cat, feet on the table. He keeps checking in with me in this subtle, secret way. He'll be talking to someone else and I'll be across the room and his eyes will dance over to mine and he keeps talking to them and looking at me and then he winks. Every so often he jumps up and gets excited about something on the yard-wide TV, rewinding the nonstop DVD of his concert so everyone can rehash the moment, like football players looking back at a game. The TV takes over the room, brighter than the glittery view out the window. You can feel the thrum of his music in your organs, and the room service keeps on coming: trays of sushi, warmed-up saki.

I'm a little worried about Moon, crouched in the doorway of the adjoining room, on a cell, keeping an eye on me and having a chat with Marley. Should he come and meet her at the party and maybe get turned away, or should she leave and meet him downtown?

Time is blurring in this pleasant claustrophobia. Like getting used to the temperature of a pool, it takes a while to adjust to the climate of a party—and a few warm sakis have helped. I go out onto the terrace, breathing in the night for what seems like just a few moments—but when I come back, I can't find the familiar landmarks: Orpheus is no longer in the huddle by the couch; Moon's not crouched in the doorway. I feel a flicker of panic, but Moon wouldn't leave me. I go to check my lipstick, and the bathroom door's locked. Back out onto the terrace, breathe in the air. Some sleazy guy looks like he's going to hit on me. Sidestep him, back into the room, and I find Moon squatting in another doorway with the phone.

I go past her with a drink in my hand, heading for the bathroom.

"Hey!" Moon says. I squat down next to her. She tells Marley to hold on a sec. To me: "Let's get out of here."

"Are you crazy? You're the one who loves him so much," I say.

"Yeah, his music. I used to like him—but look at him. . . ."

He's sitting on the thick carpet before the TV now, his head resting back on the couch. Girls lying next to him, girls draped on the arms of the couch. But he's not touching any of them.

"What's wrong with that?"

"I thought he was different, that's all. I thought he had some kind of . . . nobility, I guess." Trust Moon to use the one word that shuts you up, it's so powerful. Moon tells Marley to hang on another sec.

Orpheus isn't even looking at the girls. "They're groupies, Moon. What does that have to do with his nobility? It's not like he sleeps with them."

"Yeah, he does. . . ." To me he looks sort of innocent now, his nerdy side poking through as he leans toward the TV, eager as a kid with a video game. "Besides, so what," she says. "He's allowed to have sex. I just thought he was more cerebral—more caring. He seems so shallow. He looks like some kind of player. And I think that kid's right; he seems like he's on something."

"Moon!" Tears sting the back of my eyes. Her harshness is so sharp and clinical, like she's taking the point of a thin blade and slowly dissecting his flesh. "Why do you hate him now?"

She grabs me by the shoulders and gives me that blue-beamed inquisition. "You don't like him, do you? Nu, you better tell me—did something happen on the bus? I'm serious, tell me."

I laugh at her. "Come on, Moon, you're on drugs."

"No, but I am drunk."

"Me too."

"I'm a great sister, letting you go off with some rock star, letting you get drunk."

"Yeah you are—the best. . . ."

It's better not to argue with her. She hardly ever gets jealous of me—usually only about stuff having to do with Ma—but this is how she acts when she is. All twisted. I hate it. She's back on the phone with Marley: "Nah, we're gonna be here awhile more."

I drift pass Orpheus again and he tugs at the hem of my T-shirt. "Stay a minute, girl." He gives me that smile like we're spies together, both gathering material. It's hard to even see him: girls are all around him, either in his face or standing near him, trying to seem indifferent. I take snapshots of them in my mind, wish I had my camera. One almost six feet tall with an Indian print skirt wrapped around her skinny butt, big breasts and no bra in a white tank. Another who looks Swedish and Japanese, her skin golden, hair platinum, beautiful until she smiles and shows big-gapped teeth with jagged edges.

Guys from the band keep coming up, telling Orpheus how good he was, talking to him about particular riffs and moments only musicians notice. When Donny J switched to a minor chord, right in the middle of the—

Suddenly he reaches up and grabs me, pulling me down so I'm in an awkward kneeling position by the couch. "I've gotta deal with the fans now, you understand." He speaks low in my ear, his voice going right through me. "But later—we'll hang, right?"

"Yeah," I say, like I've done this before. Yeah, of course.

Sometime in the middle of the night, Baby Red Dread Girl shows up at the party and pulls Orpheus into the bedroom. She's pissed, and her anger gives an underlying comic note to her already gaudy outfit—she's dressed in pink and green florals, from her pillbox hat down to her pointy flats. She's yelling at Orpheus, and I move farther into the room to eavesdrop. Two girls are lying on the bed, among the summer jackets and sweaters.

She's talking about some business delivery at Constellation, scheduled for the next afternoon. "You have to be there and handle it," she says in an infant whine. "You should get to bed," she says.

"Durgha, why don't *you* go to bed?" Orpheus gives her a dismissive wave and looks over at the bed girls with a big grin, playing to an audience. "Bye-bye!"

She catches my eye then but doesn't seem to really see me through her anger. She pushes past me out the door. I think this could be my moment with Orpheus, and the coat girls try to pull him onto the bed. He resists, joking his way out of it, but I've lost my chance.

I keep heading to the bathroom because I need some-where to go. I put on more lipstick, applying it like a nervous tic.

Two girls who look younger than me are giggling to each other, pointing out famous people in the room. *A VJ from MTV, a couple of guys from Modest Mouse, that girl who played—who was it—in that vampire movie? No, that's not her. Yes it is!*

I feel a wave of superior excitement—if only they knew that I was on the bus talking to Orpheus, that he wants to hang with me later.

Moon's pissed. Had a fight with Marley and wants us to leave now. There's no way I'm going. The night goes on, my head gets blurry, the music doesn't stop. Some guy's going around telling certain people to leave, and they get out of the room reluctantly. The room's thinning out. Except for the girls; they're everywhere.

I'm waiting for my time with Orpheus.

"Hey, love, you look a little lost." He's black with a London accent, hair in neat rows. "You want something to make you feel better?" It's just like one of those peer pressure anti-drug moments. He's got E. I tell him no because I'm just too drunk, and if I mix it up I will probably die tomorrow. The phone rings and he grabs it, shielding Orpheus from all the calls.

"It's four o'clock," Moon tells me, desperate now.

"Can't *you* just go?"

"You're so obnoxious!"

I switch tactics and start softly begging.

"You're crazy," she says, but goes over to curl up on some cushions in the other room.

I know we have to go. I'm leaning into the enormous mirror looking at myself in the soft, rosy light. Take out the tube of gloss, put some on my finger, run it over my already stained and shiny mouth, splash on some green-tea-scented water from a pretty bottle next to the sink, and go back out past the girls. Something's got to happen, I can feel it.

A girl's tangled up with him on the couch. He sees me seeing her and actually peels her leg off his thigh. I can tell he's telling her to stay right there. What do I care? I don't really like him. It's not like I want to be cuddled up on the couch with him. He's hot but he's weird.

Then he's standing in front of me. "Come here for a sec," he says, pulling me into the hall by the bathroom, threading through a few people crouched there smoking pot. The bathroom door's unlocked and he pulls me in. I feel scared. More when he locks us in.

He grips my shoulders, placing me with my back against the door. His hand slides down my bare arms and the feeling flashes through me, immediate and shocking—I'm even thinking it's like a spark, it's so weird how you don't know you're attracted to someone and the touch is so sudden and—

"Shh . . . ," he says. "You're thinking too much."

I feel so exposed looking at him, his fingers curling around the belt loops of my jeans. I can feel his thumbs sliding under the waistband, the shock of that, pulling me in toward him, tight but not all the way, just close enough to make me look into his eyes.

"I love that we're the same height," he tells me, holding me there trapped, not letting our bodies touch, keeping us close enough to feel the running of each other's blood. "Only I'm much stronger." I try to pull away, want to press against him, can't do either. Torture.

He leans in like he's going to kiss me. His eyes are dark and electric. He smells so good. "Why are you so young?" he says. Then he laughs that deep laugh, breaking the spell. "Or maybe I'm just old."

Moon's sidewalk

I feel his hands relax their hold on me and I start to move and he suddenly grips me again and backs me tighter against the door. "We'll know," he says. "We'll know when the time is right." His eyes grow serious. "You are an angel, aren't you? You're like a messenger. I'm not going to let you go." But for now, he does.

***What happened?* says Moon again.** *What happened with you and Orpheus?*

We're walking in the empty night. Or morning—but still dark.

Nothing, I tell her. *Really nothing.*

Because it's true. Then why do I feel so changed?

15. Why We're Out Here

Just a saint, with tribal paint

—from "All Faces," © ORPHEUS XTIIMUSIC
(Japan import)

I'm coming out of a deep sleep, feeling the flickering, changing sunlight on my face. Dreamy thoughts of Orpheus swim up to the surface. Zack is producing his relentlessly cheerful song, and there's another sound, a fountain, water falling in a steady stream—

My eyes snap open.

"Damn, you little—!"

Taj is pissing on my floor.

Next thing I'm in the woods, gripping the leash. He's looking back with puppy exuberance and I'm wondering why we're out here when he's already done what he had to do.

16. Zen Addict

If I saw what you saw and you saw me seeing you /
maybe that place between us would disappear too

—from "I Remember That Night," © ORPHEUS XTIIMUSIC

Agnes laughing

"So when are you going to see him again?" says Agnes.

She's got shimmers of violet and green caught in the wet curls of her Afro. Sun turns all hair into prisms.

Love these endless hot days, hate the inquisition. It's late morning and we're stretched out by this rich guy's salt-water pool like we own it. Woodstock's full of so many rich people—you just have to know where they live and when they're gone; these particular rich people usually come up only on weekends.

"I know you're mesmerized by my porcelain beauty," says Agnes, "but I think I'm owed an answer. Or at least a plausible lie."

I'm sitting up in my lounge chair, sifting through the clover. Saved by the sound of a car crunching up the gravel drive.

"Man doesn't know he's a freakin' weekender," says Agnes. She shouts in the direction of the BMW: "Dude, it's Wednesday!" We grab our wet towels and head for the woods.

Late in the afternoon, Ma comes in from her own swim, carrying the dripping Taj. Her new man touches his horn; Ma shouts: "See ya later!"

To me: "Hi baby girl!" She sets Taj down and he does the dog shake thing, giving off the damp puppy smell of popcorn and dirty feet. Lumbers off to the kitchen and his doggy bowl, pausing to brush his wet furball self all over me. Zack, perched on the back of a chair, squawks in his complaining tone, flies up to the top of the fridge, the highest spot in the room, his new perch since Taj came.

Ma's dripping too, in her T-shirt over a bathing suit, all refreshed from the river.

"Have fun?" I say.

"So much." She looks like a teenager, no makeup, with that glow she gets only when she's got a new guy. "I was a little nervous swimming with him—what he'd think of my body—"

"Ma—" I can feel this heading into some queasy territory.

She plows on. "We were in the river and he goes: You have nice kids. Only I couldn't really hear what he said because the river was so loud. So I said: Thank you but you've only met one of them."

She kneels down by Taj and starts rubbing him with a towel. He treats the towel like a new toy, chewing on it, chasing it. "So he looks at me like I'm nuts and he says: I said, you have nice *tits*."

"Gross, Ma. I do not want to hear this."

"Sorry, but I thought it was funny. You don't have to be such a prude. . . ."

I take my bird and go upstairs to get ready for work.

To my right—a colony of tables needing attention.

To my left—a larger colony of the same.

In my hands: a damn heavy tray of ice water.

In my ears: "Anooshka, table thirteen still wants bread!"

Graciously deliver the water. Don't make too much eye contact. This is not about interaction.

"Anooshka, bus table seven!" Harshness from head waitress, Marian, one of those tough babes with thin, veiny arms and parentheses around her mouth.

"Yes, Marian, sorry!" Gotta kiss butt or they don't give you fifteen percent of their tips.

It's been a week since I was in the hotel with Orpheus and I think about him all the time. Wake up, there he is. All day, like a movie in my mind, playing back the scenes, hearing his voice. Being at work helps take it away—a little.

Inside the Zen Addict kitchen, the heat is on. Pans crashing and sizzling. Music blaring from a precariously balanced boom box. A fresh rust-colored stain covers the area behind the giant stoves, as if someone just threw a pot of boiled organs in a raging fit. Thor, who looks like his name, is finding it highly unlikely that the thick-lipped, dull-eyed assistant chef could graduate from the Culinary Institute producing such an interesting method of reducing basic roasted beets to a black tarry mess, gaddamit!!!!!

I'm leaving with my loaded-down water tray and stop dead when an Orpheus song, my favorite, comes on the tinny radio: *I remember that night. . . .* "Pick up for three," hisses Marian, and I move, Orpheus's voice wrapping around my heart and following me out the door.

Raphael, my hero boy, picks me up as usual.

In the jeep I try to give him ten dollars.

"No way!" We push the bill back and forth for a while. Finally I tuck it into his front jean pocket. "It doesn't even cover the gas!" I feel so bad for the guy, driving all the way to my house and then back to his house in Woodstock.

"Just promise we can have a picnic tomorrow," he says. "I never see you anymore."

"Deal."

"Well, what did you think would happen? Did you think you were going to hook up or something?"

I scoop up a cupped palm of green river water and slush it toward Raphael's face. He doesn't mind. It's only the morning and it's hot as a bitch and we're in our bathing suits on the island, up to our knees in river.

I can't stop thinking about Orpheus, and when I'm with Raphael I can't shut up about him. We keep reviewing what happened at the party. Analyzing his character. And there are things I can't convey to Raph— the quiet little play of intimacy on the tour bus, the chaotic surge inside when he grabbed me and held me, the way he looked at me and told me *I'm not going to let you go*.

I keep going online to feel his mind, rekindle his presence. The only time I feel free of him is on the island.

"What did you want from him, anyway?"

There is a perfect word for Raphael:

Artless.

It is almost the opposite of what it seems to be. At least to me, artless sounds like something cloddish and clumsy and mass marketed. Actually it means something that is effortlessly beautiful, uncontrived, and unrehearsed.

There he is with that perfect bronze-colored body, looking like a rock star or *GQ* model in his faded, shredded shorts and his silly turquoise glasses, but he's as unselfconscious as a puppy, beautiful the way toddlertots are beautiful. Sometimes I just look at him as if he's a work of art, but usually I take it for granted, especially when I'm annoyed with him, like *right now*!

"I mean, do you want to raise little rock star babies with him?"

"No, I want us to *e-mail* each other!"

The stupidity of my remark, no matter how completely true it is, shuts us both up, and we sit there in a kind of mutual awe and horror.

I lie straight out on my stomach on the hot, flat rock, covering my head with my sun hat, feeling the sweat run down the back of my ears, down my neck.

"Did you really just say that?" he says eventually.

"Well, it's true. I feel like we're friends having a one-way conversation. I read his diaries and I want to write back to him."

"Why don't you just blog on his website, like everybody else?"

"Exactly. Like everybody else. Please, you know I'm not an idiot. I'm not a stalker. Am I?"

"No, you big dope, you're not a stalker," he says in a comforting tone, patting my back. I start to relax. "You don't read his diary four times a day and you didn't go to the city to find him and Santa *will* be here with that dolly you want . . . and—*gross!* Your back is all sweaty!"

Tell him to shut up. Sit up and hug my knees. Use a rock to dig at a hard, sticky, dead bug that looks like a tiny black crab, dried onto the surface of the rock.

A couple floats past in inner tubes, holding hands, silent, eyes closed. Hidden in the reeds and cattails, we are mute, watching them. Raph and I exchange a shifty spy-eyed glance, the one we developed back when we were seven and first played Spy. When you are friends forever, days of talking can be distilled into a secret gesture, five words, one look.

"I just don't get the whole deal with Orpheus," Raph says.

"Maybe if you keep asking me a thousand questions, you'll get it."

Except it's not really fair to expect him to understand this Orpheus thing when I don't.

I come home late in the afternoon, to an empty house—except for Taj crooning to me pitifully behind the baby gate in the kitchen. While I'm fastening on his leash, I find a note from Ma: Spending night at Frank's house. Froz. lasagne in freezer. Please walk Taj. XOXOXOXOXO

She possesses me when it's convenient for her, using me to fill her emptiness, runs away when she feels like it, leaving me to care for her damn dog.

When I call Moon later, she's in the ranting mode about Marley. Says he's making her claustrophobic.

If this is love, it sucks.

I haven't felt that *thing* they all talk about and *I don't want to*. I have seen my mother go through it so many times and my sister.

This is how it is with my mother: she meets a man and does not even like him at first. This is the crucial first step: an initial contempt or disgust.

I hate it when she comes home late at night from a party and says: I met this guy, what an arrogant jerk.

Watch out. Two days later she is saying: Wow, as it turns out, he's actually sweet. He's really nice. He's taking me to dinner. Suddenly there is an Amazing Connection between them. He loves Italian movies from the sixties *just like she does*. They *both absolutely adore* deciduous trees! Wow, what a match made in heaven! What destiny! She now has no ability to resist his charms.

At this point he stops calling. She seeks my counsel. Do I think he meant this when he said that. Do I think she was too aggressive when she did that last week. Can she just tell me the dream she had about him early that morning, which has given her insight into why he might have neglected to give her a kiss good night on their last date. Why can't she? Is it too much to ask that I just listen to her for a few damn minutes?

And then she goes to a new therapist or her South American healer and the healer spits chewed-up herbs into her belly button or whatever and then she's okay for a few weeks until the next dude she hates comes along and surprises her by being her True Destiny. Or else she just spends 9,022 hours on the computer and comes home with a bear cub for me to take care of.

And then there is ZZ Moon. She is nothing like Ma, and yet I have heard them agree with each other on a few little points:

Ma: You can never let a man see who you really are.

The Z GIRL: You're right about that one.

Ma: And don't ever spend more than twenty-four hours with him.

Moonster: No way. Gotta throw him out after the first night.

Ma: They want you as long as you don't need them.

Z: But they want to be helpful and take care of you. Still, you gotta tell them to leave you alone; you're fine on your own.

Ma: And you have to really be fine. You have to be tough. It helps if he sort of annoys you and you really don't want him around too much. Then they go crazy.

Z: The best thing is if you're interested in someone else and thinking about the other guy all the time.

Ma: Then they really fall for you.

Z: But as soon as you fall for them, they're gone.

Ma: They're out of there.

I've seen them sobbing in each other's arms. A few winters ago, when Z was just sixteen, they both broke up with their guys right before the holidays. The house was decorated in misery! I came home from school to this:

Ma: It felt so good.

Z: I know, it was the best day of my life.

Ma: When I'm with him, it's like a drug.
Z: I feel like I'm home.

It sounded like they were talking about the same guy. Infatuation. For me, this will never happen. I will never think like that. Pasting feelings onto any handy person. Ma and ZZ Moon were like junkies giving themselves fixes, only instead of the needles they used humans.

That was the last time Ms. Z got her heart broken. And now she's already getting bored with Marley. It's only been a few days since I saw the love doves in the city and Moon's on the phone with me, saying *I am getting the minty fresh feeling.* That's our code for when she becomes too aware of the guy's anything. She used to tune in to the guy's breath. She had one guy who she said smelled like old bamboo and another one whose breath smelled like moth balls in an attic in June. She gets so specific. Finally she said she hated all breath, even minty fresh breath.

I'm sitting on my bed with my legs propped up and Zack balanced on my big toe, singing his heart out. I ask Moon exactly what it is that's bothering her about Marley.

He has this vulnerable look.

That sounds cute.

Believe me, it's not. It's nauseating.

Can't you just ignore it?

I doubt it.

I thought you adored him.

Not anymore. He's changed.

Are you sure, Moon? Maybe you're just afraid of getting too close.

Maybe he's just too nauseating.

Right. After all, she is right. I always thought he was excessive and nauseating. And the tattoos by his eye are so corny.

He's probably the kind of guy if you really liked him back, he'd be a dick, I tell her.

You are so right, she says. Thanks, Nu-nu.

Sure, Moonie.

At least we get each other.

Even if I can't talk to her about Orpheus, the same way I can't talk to Raphael about Orpheus.

So how's Orpheus? she asks me.

Great, I say.

Is he calling every day?

Twice, I say. Sometimes even three times.

Lucky girl!

Yeah, except he's been getting that vulnerable look a lot lately. It makes my skin crawl.

It's a bitch, ain't it.
Oh yeah, Moon, it is.

Even though they're cynical, my mother and sister are basically romantics—and they have all their hopes pinned on me. It's going to be different for you, they tell me in so many ways.

17. On Tour

You are never more alone than in a hotel room

—from "Always There," © ORPHEUS XTIIMUSIC

He has less than a week left on his tour. The rain's pounding outside my window, and I imagine it coming down outside his hotel room, too. I can see him in pinstriped pj's, seated before his laptop at a fake wood desk in the room. Sartre's *Nausea* open on his bed. There are towels on the floor. The windows are open, and the hotel faces a parking lot, rain collecting in oily pools on the asphalt.

Orpheus Online

we always go to a hotel with 350 orange triangles on the carpet, three packets of instant high-end coffee, the same beige ice bucket to the right of the bed, the same painting of a lovely farmhouse above the TV, even the lumps in the pillows to be found in the same place. the sameness makes me able to pretend . . .

I see him on his bed now, staring at the ceiling. . . .

> . . . that a thousand strangers have not slept in this bed before me, maybe leaving traces that are still somewhere in the room. closing my eyes, thinking of the rhythm of the road, opening them to see the permanently closed windows — closing them, opening — and then — finally shutting the light. good night and sleep tight to you.

I'm out in the dark and the rain, walking the mongrel on my river road, but feeling myself in Orpheus's room, telling him he's not alone. I imagine him opening his eyes one more time and, in the darkness, sensing me.

I'm dipping a wilted fry into mustard at the food court in the mall with Ma. Packages are heaped around us.

"I don't know what it is," the drama queen's saying. "Did I do something? Did something happen in your life?"

This has been going on throughout the day, and there's no point in speaking.

"You've changed."

I try mixing a little hot sauce with the mustard. No improvement.

"We could've had a great afternoon together. But you're so cold. You're not even excited about the new shoes I got you!"

"I didn't ask you to get them, Ma." Bitchy, but I can't resist. How many times have I told her I don't really care about shoes?

"You are so cold!" She's hissing with intensity. "We're a family, damn it. Even if it's a family of two! It's just us, and you need to communicate."

A few girls I know from school are passing by, checking us out.

"Ma, would you stop?"

"No, I'm not stopping."

Fine. I pick up my stuff and head out the main entrance to the car.

She's crying on the highway and veers into someone's lane and gets cursed out. I look at Ma and almost feel sorry for her—the tears are real. I'm about to say something nice, force myself, and then—

"Jesus, what's that stink?"

I look in the backseat. Sure enough. "Bad dog!" I tell Taj.

Ma starts cracking up. "Not his fault! We shoulda walked him."

"We?"

Ma is laughing hard.

"What is so funny?" I tuck my shirt over my nose.

"I can't help it—bad smells make me laugh."

I make a huge effort to keep my rage, but I start cracking up. "Yeah, me too."

In the middle of all this joy and goodwill I ask her sweetly if I can go to the city tomorrow. Miracle of miracles, the answer is yes.

Later, I'm with Agnes at her grandma Benita's place. She's just out of the hospital and we're making her a batch of food. We're all sitting in the little kitchen while split pea soup simmers on the stove. (Lots of carrots, onions, and celery, and Benita's secret ingredients: dash of liquid smoke and pinch of fragrant cardamom.) Benita tastes the hot soup, sipping from a wooden spoon. I watch her deftly moving a steaming pot of veggies without a pot holder. She catches my awe and laughs. "Asbestos fingers!" she says.

She has the shiniest polished wood floor in her kitchen. Sometimes I purposely drop things onto it just for the joy of wiping it up so easily.

Masks stare out from every free space—Chinese theater masks, ceremonial and tribal ones, even the painted plaster ones Agnes and her little brother made of their own faces in elementary school. She keeps thanking us for helping, but we can barely get her to sit down with her tea.

"So why do you keep going back to the city?" Benita asks. "It's gotta be a guy."

"Exactly, dude," says Agnes. Benita is cool. How many

grandmas can you call "dude"?

Benita wraps herself tighter in her floppy sweater and gives me a hard stare. "Once you start chasing a guy, the game is off balance," she says. "Nobody's going to win."

I start to protest that I'm not chasing him, but I get this uneasy feeling that I am. "I just have to see him now that he's back from a tour," I tell them. "And that'll be it—the last time." They both give slow nods in response, like skeptical twins.

Early the next morning, good-bye to Zack. Whistle to him in soft bird twitter, raising him close to my face. His feet are curled around my finger and he's got his head cocked, twittering back. I nuzzle his soft head against my cheek. An enormous love sweeps through me. *Oh, Zackie,* I tell him. His eyes hold so much kindness. I want to say more—*I adore you, sorry I have to go,* but the understanding between us is our language. I set him gently on top of his cage.

In the cab, on my cell with Moon. Hear her getting rid of a customer at the CD place where she works.

"I can't believe you're doing this," she tells me. "Again. And it's dangerous to be in this heat. . . ."

The cab's air-conditioned but outside the air's bent with waves of heat. The streets are almost empty; the few people walking are practically naked, shielded under umbrellas, pressing ice to their sweaty faces and necks, moving in slo-mo.

"I like it hot," I tell her. "Besides, he got back from his tour yesterday, and he has to be there. He loves that place; it's like his home. Where else would he be?"

18. Looking for My Boy

Hot, crazed, and stupid / stumbling in your wake /
hot, crazed, and stupid / what a twisted fate /
i'll go and find you anywhere coz I adore you, yeah, I care

—from "Always There," © ORPHEUS XTIIMUSIC

Early in the afternoon, and the roof of Constellation is a baked tar mess. A few people in the shade by the plants. Top edge of the skyline wavering in the inferno. No Orpheus.

Back inside, the heat is less intense, but there's still a sticky, tropical feeling in the air and the cloying smell of bananas. I grab an empty table by the bar where a girl's whirring a blender drink. I keep hearing the warning of the emergency weather advisory. *Don't go outside unless absolutely necessary.* This seemed so necessary, but now the urgency seems to have evaporated.

I'm so tired I want to lay my head on the table, but I don't want to look weird. I already feel so obvious. Look at the poster girl for pathetic, in her pink high-tops and safari hat, looking for Orpheus. And there's Durgha,

I recognize her little face, even though her baby dreads are gone. She's wearing a tank top cut off just under her breasts with her pale, pierced torso exposed. Her hair is cut two inches from the scalp and her sharp-boned face shimmers with perspiration. I'm watching her like she's on TV, listening to her strained, brisk voice as she gives instructions to the blender girl: *And then after you prep the carrots . . . make sure the ice is not stacked on top of the . . . and do not put the tomatoes in the . . .*

She comes out from the bar carrying a plate of food. She has blue dents under her eyes. Not even a flicker of recognition as she moves past my table, delivering the food to a table by the window. But of course she doesn't know me—she only saw me twice, on the roof before the concert and at the hotel after-party, when she was pissed and I probably looked like just any of a thousand fans.

The place is so busy. My stomach goes tight when I spot dark hair and a baseball cap—no, and then another—no—. Funny there's so many of them, like clones gone wrong. My stomach is fluttery, but I order a little salad. A $16.97 salad! I run my fingertips over the scratched, yellowish wood of the table. It reminds me of an old school desk that's been sanded down; I try to read some of the faded graffiti. *Jogimba sucks.* Yeah, I bet he, she, or it does suck. If only I had a book or magazine, but I never go to places like this alone, so how could I think of that? Moon, where are you?

Two beautiful, long-legged girls next to me are having a gross conversation.

"I wanted to wear sandals but my toenails are like yellow," says the girl in a purple-flowered tiny tank dress. They're the kind of girls that look great from not too far away. Zoom in on them and they are not all that. They keep craning their necks to see if Orpheus will show up.

"I heard that's from some kind of fungus," says the Asian girl, who's sitting with her white chiffon skirt rolled up, exposing her slender thighs. Why are those thighs exposed? For my Orpheus? I don't think he would like that. But maybe he would.

The girls are sitting practically inches away from me and are acting like there's some kind of sound barrier between us.

"Ryan wants me, I'm serious. He is always like, I want to marry you so bad. And I'm always like, I don't at all. Pretty much we're just friends."

"Except when you accidentally gave him that rubdown naked."

We get our food at the same time. Ingredients arranged on a giant white plate. Microscopic cubes of red peppers, yellow squash, and cucumber in an intricate pattern around a steamed artichoke heart with a drizzle of red pepper dressing. Pixilated food. I have no appetite. I have no plan.

Then Durgha brings in her laptop and parks herself at a nearby table. She's sitting with a European-looking chick in her twenties or so. She has the same high-cut chopped do as Durgha's, only hers is tortoiseshell colored.

Orpheus's best gal pal is sitting next to us and the two girls at the other table go right on, jabbering and clueless. Wish Raph could admire this spy work!

"Ave you talked to heem today?" French accent from Tortoiseshell Woman.

"No, and I'm just a little bit worried," says Durgha. "Usually he e-mails me first thing in the afternoon when he gets up. I guess he's tired. They just got back from the tour last night."

This is too good. But where is he? He might not show at all. I didn't realize how much I'd been operating like some kind of robot on an Orpheus track. Reading his diary. Thinking about him all day as if our minds were connected. Racing to the city before he leaves for his tour . . . I didn't imagine us not connecting.

"Eet ese zo beezey ear," says French Girl. "You must bee zo appee."

"It's good, I guess. But we were supposed to just have

these amazing drinks. Orpheus is the one who's crazy about the food. He keeps wanting to add more food to the menu, and I wish we just had like bar snacks."

The blender gets going again at the bar and I can't hear them for a few moments. The smell of bananas and kiwis wafts from the bar and the place feels so daytime and flat like any place in the universe. I haven't heard any music since I got off the elevators. Close your eyes and you could be in a mall food court. She could be talking about some bossy, middle-aged restaurant owner instead of a rock star.

Every so often the massive front door opens and little crowds trickle in. Some of the people crane their necks the second they get in, squinting for a glimpse of *him*.

A couple in matching British Isles T-shirts heads toward the bar. The girl gazes past me, squeezes her boyfriend's arm and says: "I saw Orpheus sitting right at that bar last night!"

I suck in my breath. So he was here. How could I have not felt it. . . .

"No, bitch, you did not," says Durgha, quietly and cheerfully so she thinks only her friend can hear. Oblivious to her dig, the couple sits down at the far end of the bar. "He wasn't even here last night," Durgha tells her pal. And adds, as an insightful additional commentary: "Fuckin' ho."

Wow, Ms. Evolved. Does Orpheus know she speaks like that? Of course, they are pals; he knows everything. He helps her take out her garbage. She whines to him about all her wretched boyfriends. She even calls him up when her nail breaks. They lean on each other in bed, watching TV. I don't know how I know that, but it is absolutely true. It doesn't matter how she talks or what she says. They have a real deep love.

Inside Constellation

Abruptly, I feel disconnected from all the objects in the room, everything within my vision, including my empty water glass, my own hands, and the sticky yellow wood of the table. I feel like I have been unplugged from the world, sitting there in a private, lost freak-out while everything moves on as usual, making sense to all the people—sitting, talking, planning, drinking, with their eyeballs, nostrils, digestive tubes, their weird sounds passing from their mouth tubes into ear tubes. It's déjà vu gone wrong. The door opens to the roof, letting in a thick gust of heat. I have a quick glimpse of the sky, and even that has an off-kilter appearance. It looks like a blank screen.

I pay for my lunch and leave, making myself walk even though I'm so light-headed my face feels like it's floating a few inches off my body. I'd considered our connection so inevitable that I never imagined the possibility that I wouldn't see him.

On the street the heat is more than I remembered. A black dog is collapsed panting on the sidewalk. The street sign for the next block seems like a far-off landmark. If I keep walking, if we are really connected, we will find each other. He is coming this way, I am going his way, I know it. My longing to see him snaps me back into reality. The heat becomes a beautiful monster. The city speaks in sensory pulses: the burned vanilla smell of giant lilies in an outdoor flower stand, a nun catching my eye, a cell phone ringing with a mechanical Russian tune, the sharp smell of urine, an old man with a saggy red face at the newspaper stand. All clues about Orpheus, somehow.

I head out toward the Bowery, passing little kosher

dairy places, thrift stores, shoe stores where the drag queens shop. The heat forces me to stop in at least one store on every block, to keep from fainting. But what if we miss each other while I am inside? No, it can't happen. Whatever needs to happen will happen if you let it. I am moving through a rack of glittery net tops in operatic tropical colors, fingering each one, trying to make the coolness of the store last.

All I want is an acknowledgment that he feels it too. There could be a greater part of us that comes out when we sleep or daydream, that exists above us in the atmosphere, guiding our actions like an ethereal movie director. I imagine my director conspiring with his, leading both of us through the maze of the city: turn left now, slow down, now turn right, smile at that nun, step past the lilies, open the door, and you will find each other. . . . Wasn't that how people ran into each other, against all odds? Find me, I'm thinking. Find me.

Standing outside the Bowery Mission. The double doors are flung open. Deep inside, beneath a statue of Christ, four women are making the air vibrate with gospel. A few dozen people are scattered on the benches, some of them wildly into the service. A guy rushes in to shake a homeless person. No sleeping, the guy tells him. I keep on going.

Lower Broadway—cheap shopping paradise. Everything

is on *sale*. I might find a cool bathing suit for four bucks. That can happen. Or funky London sunglasses. A stupid necklace with a red dog. Things like that. I go into a Swedish chain store. Throngs of people, three stories, stuff spilling out of bins and hanging crookedly, all picked through, from the racks. Club music, so loud it massages your heart. Hate it! I head toward the exit and—

—there they are.

The two long-legged gals who sat next to me at Constellation. Happily grabbing stuff off the racks.

What the hell.

What are the chances.

Why them.

Why not him.

What does it mean.

Apparently nothing.

I walk past them. Stand in front of them. Stare right at them. They do not know me. They are so dead of the head they probably didn't even notice me when I sat next to them. Or maybe they have already said to each other, hey, there's the losergirl who sat next to us at lunch. But I doubt it. They are not awake. I look around at all the faces, all the buyers. Everyone is in their own world. No one is looking at anyone else.

Okay, if that's the way it's going to be, I'll get away from the heat and the stink, go to a museum. Climb onto the first uptown bus, settle into my sticky seat, grateful for the weak air-conditioning. It's not until we're lurching through midtown traffic that I realize my whole mission fizzled out and I'm headed away from any chance to run into Orpheus.

19. Oh Yeah, Trees, a Nude, How Nice

*I like their green lips and the way they sip coffee /
they can't see me but I know they would like me*

—from "Maybe I Do Have Friends," © ORPHEUS XTIIMUSIC
with Comet Pearson

Way too many people have escaped the heat to be inside,
staring at Gauguin's tropical paintings.

The colors of Tahiti look surprisingly dark and
subdued—from what I can glimpse through the knotted
limbs of the onlookers. Earthen shades—browns, ambers,
toned-down turquoise—instead of screaming pinks and
glowing oranges. Maybe the paint faded. There are so
many people hungry for Gauguin, they stand two per
painting all along the main corridor and in several rooms.

I was probably not old enough to talk when my father
first took me to a gallery and showed me how to look into
paintings, to make them melt. I still see paintings as frozen
panels of reality.

It's do-it-yourself cloning; instead of building a being

out of a crumb of DNA, you're unlocking breath from a petrified piece of art. But you can't just look at the thing and say oh yeah, trees, a nude, a red umbrella, how nice. You have to let your mind receive its essence.

I can't get near all the really well known Gauguin paintings, so I go into the smallest room, which also has his drawings. An old guy stands before a painting of a Tahitian woman with his wife, who has long black hair and a straw hat and honey-colored skin. Tenderly, the guy says look, that's you.

There's a tiny drawing next to them with plenty of room. I stand there and no one bothers me.

At first I don't get much from it. A guy with pointy devilish eyes and muppetlike sprouts of hair sits hunched over an apple. A few books lie in front of him and you can read the titles. One of them is *Paradise Lost* by Milton.

A card beside the drawing gives a brief background: The guy was a friend of Gauguin's. His name was Meyer de Haan and he was also a painter, and he hooked up with one of Gauguin's lovers, an innkeeper named Marie.

I keep looking at the drawing and then the scene starts to thaw and, by looking at what Gauguin saw, I begin to realize that Gauguin's heart was broken—but in a cranky, non-sentimental, sarcastic way. Gauguin once had paradise with Marie—a cute, white-toothed, energetic woman who was a fabulous cook. And this Meyer de Haan came along, like the devil, like the snake in the garden of Eden, and took it all away. But in the end Gauguin didn't really want Marie. After all, he was still married and had five or six kids with some other woman.

So Gauguin sat there and sketched his pal and felt sort of sad about the past, but not really. He actually liked the chance to whine and complain about the past; and then he felt free to turn his pal into a devilish caricature.

It takes a while to crack the code, but when it happens, it comes in an obvious, sudden rush. I know these things as clearly as if they are being played out on a TV soap opera in front of my eyes. I draw a little picture of the picture in my notebook so I can bring it out and thaw it at home.

Alone in Moon's apartment. I think I'm getting used to the heat. I have always loved heat. The way it covers everything, the way you can almost see it, the way you feel so proud of yourself that you are surviving it. Those summer nights are the best, when the dark air touches your face gently, like it's ten in the morning. I love the way you have to move slowly and wear less clothes, and I love how people bond together in the crises of a heat wave, everyone happy to be suffering from the identical plague.

Only now it's just me and a jar of mayo, a perfect avocado, half a tomato, a sliver of mozzarella, and some nice, squishy Jewish rye bread. And a ton of salt. It is an amazing sandwich. I never get to buy my own food at home. If I use my own money for food, it's usually for pizza or taco crap at the mall. I would never buy some cheese and stuff and bring it home. Ma would be like: What are you doing? Or else she would eat it herself. She would say thank you for bringing me some food for a change. You never know what she would do, actually, but the food definitely would not sit calmly in the fridge, faithfully waiting for me.

And pepper. Tons of cracked black pepper, ground on with the tall pepper mill. ZZ Moon is so cool to have things like pepper mills.

I make a humongous sandwich and sit with it at her pink, fake marble kitchen counter. There's an inspiring view out the tall, open window of a gray brick wall. From the street there's a horn, a shout, a whooping car alarm that won't stop. This sandwich is ecstasy.

The phone rings.

I know it's Ma.

She'll want to talk to Moon if I answer, to make sure Moon is with me every second. So I don't answer. My private rule with Moon: I am not allowed to go out anywhere in the city alone after dark unless she has approved. No problem. There is nowhere I like to go by myself at night. And usually I hook up with Moon anyway.

Machine picks up.

"Hello?" says Ma, tentatively. "Hello, Moonie, Anooshka Star? Can anyone hear me?"

Yes, I tell the air. (Little pang of guilt.)

"It's dinnertime so I guess you're out having something delicious."

Yup, I say. Yup, we are.

"Whatever you're doing, I hope you girls are having a wonderful time!" (Bigger guilt pang.)

We're doing crack, Ma.

"This is your mother." The ultimate Ma thing. Like we'd think it was a freaking solicitor.

"Okay, sweetie pies, I love you! Call me!"

Big relief. I turn on the stereo to blast away the guilt.

Orpheus, of course. Singing a slower song, good for my digestion.

What a damn great sandwich. Some Indian healer guy said that you should do nothing else but eat when you are eating. I like to eat, watch vintage *Real World*s, listen to music, and read a mag at the same time. Tonight I will just sit and chew. I take my sandwich over to Moon's tiny cute writing desk. Okay, turn on her laptop. It's his first day back from tour; he will have to write something. Even if he writes about sleeping all day, I have to know how the heck he spent the day while I was searching the world for him.

Orpheus Online
New York

he once had marie's scent pounded into his heartbeat. a
breath of milk, like a baby's breath, breathed lightly on top of
the mildest perfume of violets and clover. once, anything
vaguely linked with milk — mowed april grass, for example,
or a sun-warmed cowhide — would raise his heart in his chest.
more moving than her scent was the way she quickly pulled
in her lips with fear or before she laughed. in the mornings
while she bathed, he went outside, tired and almost dizzy in
the sun, to crush sun-scorched basil between his thick painted
fingers in her garden and he would wear the sad scent of herb
and wet dirt all day, reminding him of the meal she'd made
at 3 a.m. when they ate naked in her kitchen. he was afraid
there would not be another meal like it but the next night it
would be prepared again and they would laugh again and sit
naked in the kitchen. all summer long. no one in the world
had her thin fingers and tiny nails and narrow wrists or such a
waist contained so neatly within a starched white blouse.
these things were embroidered into his heart. a thousand colored lines from his heart to outside triggers in the world,
strings pulled all day long, producing joy or sharp pain. that is
how it once was but now there is only a fondness left. now
when he paints her lover, the one she chose over him, it is
an intellectual exercise, not done as catharsis, deep pain, shooting stars of passion. he sits with her lover, his pal, under

two old paintings in the dining room of m's place. so many years have passed. this is how civilized things can become. this is proof of time's transformative powers. you don't have to die and be born again to work out karma with your rivals. they sit beneath the familiar old paintings and gauguin peers at his friend with the thin orange hair and red mottled face, the man he calls the orange dutch jew and thinks how good the orange would look next to a hot yellow and a purple pink. . . .

"you are thinking my face green, aren't you," says the dutch jew.

"no, pink," says gauguin.

the air this early evening is moist, almost cool. a clatter from the kitchen. green light from high windows through dense tree leaves.

the coffee is burned somehow. a delicious smell of shallots in butter. a plate of glistening sweaty grapes.

"those grapes are too sweet," says the dutch jew.

"for you, maybe," says gauguin. "not sweet enough for me." the dutch jew stares at him. "i get it now," he says. "you're painting me again as the devil."

"egomaniac," says gauguin. "why would i ever paint you agaln?"

gauguin sips the black coffee. it's not the coffee that's burned, it's his tongue. how good meyer de haan will look with red pointy eyes, gauguin thinks. on his friend's transparent white throat, a blue vein pulses, giving gauguin a fleeting tender feeling and also making him hungry for eggs and ham. the next day the drawing is done.

20. Darling Strangers

Back in the city

Pack your toothbrush and come with me

—from "Flying Carpet," © ORPHEUS XTIIMUSIC

"You don't understand; it was the *same* painting."

"I told you I get it." Moon says each word like it ends with a period. "I just think you're making a really big deal about it."

I made Moonie and her guy come and meet me at the

falafel place near Moon's. Couldn't stay inside my own skin after reading the diary. Nobody wants to get a table, but nobody wants to hit the hot streets, so we're just hanging by the video games at the entrance.

"Maybe she has OCD," Marley says, slipping three more quarters into a sparring zombie machine. He has the most expressionless eyes I have ever seen in my life. They're sorta pretty, pale green. And they have those tattooed stars at the corners. But no matter what he says, his eyes are always the same.

I whack him in the arm. He turns those blank eyes on me. "Yow."

"I do not have OCD!"

"You've talked about it from the second we got here and all through five games. You can't shut up about it, so—"

"Okay, enough," says ZZ Moon. "Marley, I wish you could be a little more—I don't know, you're just so harsh about everything."

Good! She's starting to have the minty fresh thing in a major way. I'm getting sick of the blank-eyed rag boy myself.

"Moon," I say softly, trying not to let Marley hear, "don't you think it's amazing that we both have the same theory about looking at paintings and finding out their deeper meanings?"

"Sweetie, I don't mean to be patronizing, but people who are into art do that." So much for the minty fresh thing. Not on my side, either. "People spend hours looking at paintings, searching for symbols and stuff."

"But Moon, you always get what I'm talking about. Why can't you get this? We saw the same thing when we looked at the painting. Can't you understand that? Don't you think that's an amazing coincidence?"

She bumps my forehead with hers, and instead of doing its calming trick, our code gesture totally pisses me off. "Great works of art have universal messages," she says.

"Moon, cut the shit."

"But they do . . . maybe it's not so easy for everyone to see the same message, I mean maybe you and Orpheus are extra sensitive, and smart—"

"And extra psychotic," says Marley. "Tripping out on paintings." His guy dies with a little mechanical whine and Marley gives a farewell smack to the machine.

"But we were both in the same museum on the same day." I'm gripping Moon's shoulders, on the verge of shaking her. "Seriously, what are the chances of that?"

"Yeah, it's unusual," Moon says, casually slipping out from my grasp. "But not totally freaky. I mean, I wouldn't take it as this amazing sign."

"Ob-sessive, com-pulsive, dis-order," Marley says happily. "You're obsessed and you can't stop yourself. Takes one to know one!" He takes a vampire bite of Moonie's golden brown neck and pulls a thrilled scream out of her.

One second back in that hot night and all we want to do is find some air-conditioned joint. None of us has much money, but Marley knows a place on Seventh Avenue with cheap iced coffee and free refills. As we cross Eighth Avenue, where the street is narrow and not well lit, a little boy grabs our attention. He's inside a grassy area with three scrawny trees and a bunch of flowers. There's a chain-link fence around it and he's running like crazy with a glass jar, looking through the flower beds.

"Hey," he calls to us. "Have you seen a little mouse?"

There's an old grandfatherly-looking guy in a sleeveless undershirt leaning up against a car. "Are you with him?" I ask him.

"Yes," he says in a thick accent. "I am the grandpapa."

"Did he lose his pet, or is he trying to catch a rat or something?" I ask.

"Yes!" says the old guy.

I get up close to the chain link. The boy is beautiful. Dusky skin, curly dark hair, nearly black eyes, small, maybe seven. He's leaping around the enclosure like a flying reindeer, speed-talking to his imaginary mouse, alternately all tender and then twisted. "Where did you go, mousie mousie? I need a pet, damn it. Get back here, you scum mouse."

"Come on!" Marley tells me. "Let's go, dude."

"Yeah, Anooshka, it's gross out here, let's go."

We get totally wired on a bunch of flavored watery coffees. We invent a few new games involving spilled piles of coarse brown sugar and coffee stirrers. I get vibrant as a preacher on the caffeine and almost convince Marley and Moon that the whole Gauguin episode is amazing. We leave the place and walk back the way we came to get a subway downtown.

The boy is still there.

So is the grandfather.

Don't start, Moon says.

But I can't believe they're still here, I say.

OCD, baby, Marley sings in tune to an old Jackson Five song, "ABC."

You think I'm sick just because I notice things, because I'm interested in people?

Moon's hand on my shoulder. The grandfather giving me the proud grandpa look.

Did you find him? I ask the boy.

His frenetic movement stops and he looks me dead in the eyes. *Obviously not,* he says. Explodes back into action, monologuing to himself. How could he have done this for an hour? Did he really say *obviously not?*

We're leaving, Moon says, way too gently.

I don't talk to them on the subway. Maybe I am losing it. They say a big sign of mental illness is not knowing you have it. But isn't it real insanity to go through the world ignoring the people in front of you? All your friends were strangers before they became friends. I sneak glances at the darling strangers on the subway.

"You sure you're okay to be by yourself tonight?"

They've walked me to her door. Totally unnecessary.

"I could send Marley off. I don't have to spend every single night with him. . . ."

Marley, the gorgeous caveboy, jeans in tatters, is plucking at the hem of Moon's lilac and lime chiffon mini. Tug, tug. Like a little toddlertot. *Come awn,* he says. *Moonie, come aaw-on, grrrll.*

I always think of old people when I walk up the five steep flights. What do they do when they're stuck up high and their limbs don't work?

The heat hangs on like a spirit. I turn the key in Moon's lock and even before I flip the light switch, her empty apartment shocks me by being just the way I left it. Everything that hits my sight—the sandwich plate and mayo knife in the sink, the dark computer, the open window, the still-damp purple towel hanging over the back of a chair—everything still jangles with my excitement. Before I left I was spinning; but after a night of being told that I was an obsessed lunatic, coming back to this place is so humbling, like meeting a younger version of myself. How amazing that you can think you are experiencing a profound happening, almost like a miracle—and then you realize that you just made it that way in your mind.

I feel so worn out from the day, almost sad enough to cry. I turn off the overhead light and plug in a red paper lamp on the writing table; it gives the room a lurid glow. I put on the radio. No Orpheus now, thank you. Something melancholy and dark. A woman singing. I take a few fake modern spins around the room; doesn't matter if the neighbors across the way see. It's so hot. I pick up the phone. Maybe I'll call Raphael—no, don't want to run Moon's bill up. I go to the computer. I won't put it on; I just like sitting at her desk. Yeah, right. I turn it on; I'll only check my e-mail. Uh-huh, sure. Log on to Orpheus. He might write twice in one day. Sometimes he does. Holding my breath in that two-beat pause, and the moment his diary appears, my heart wedges like a wild bird in my throat, as if he had just stepped into the room.

Orpheus Online
New York

i'm so happy to be back. museums by day and walking the streets at night. (not one person recognized me; it's a little humbling.) there's such a balmy, slow mood in the city tonight. am i the only one who sometimes feels oh so sad when you see certain strangers and realize you will never see them again — and even if you did see them again, even if you became the best of friends, you would never know that you had once passed them on the street. somehow that seems wrong.

one of the best things about being back is i get to eat at constellation. i'm heading there now. . . .

good night, wherever you are.

Okay. I say it out loud, like I've just been given a directive. Okay, one, he has the stranger thing like I do. He had it on the same day! And two, he has announced to the world his immediate destination. It's so obvious. Even the blinking cursor on the screen seems to be in synch with some kind of new slow-motion perfect universe.

Then the calm shatters and I'm on my feet, pacing. What now. There's some kind of channel between us. I know it. I'm sure he knows it, even if he doesn't know it's me yet. What now. I look out the window facing the street, press my head against the dirty glass. He's got to sense me at the other end. What, what. It's such a cool feeling, like having a psychic twin. And then he comes out and says where he's going to be. Won't that draw throngs of people to the place? Yeah, maybe he needs business. Or maybe he just wants to see that one person who he knows is out there and connected to his heart in some way. So *move*, girl!

I tear through my backpack for loose change. Okay, I have a return bus ticket. Moon'll lend me dough. I find almost ten dollars. That's so not enough. I don't care. I'm out of here. Look at my wild face in the mirror. I'm fine, I'm fine. I'm wearing the same stinking pink high-tops, rag of a T-shirt, a boring denim skirt. Check the Hello Kitty clock on the wall. Almost eleven. It doesn't matter, *move*. Get out that door and down those stairs. *No*, take those shoes off, wash your feet quick in the tub. Put on a pair of Moon's black sandals that lace halfway up the leg. Way too goth with the skirt. It doesn't matter. It's all okay. It's all going to happen. It's going to happen like there's a ten-foot-tall neon arrow pointing to it.

It doesn't even hit me how bad I am until I'm in a cab three blocks along in the ride. The air-conditioning's broken and the windows are down, letting in the hot, black night. I am watching the meter like it's a heart monitor. I don't have enough money to get there. I'm not supposed to be going anywhere. I have no cab fare back. I feel light-headed and surreal like someone else has made all this happen. I've got to at least save two bucks for phone calls or whatever. "Here," I tell the driver, ten blocks from Constellation.

I pay him and fly out the door. It's so good to be out alone. Not scary at all. Lots of couples on the street, everyone out for fun. Summer good mood. No really whacked people here. I walk quickly. I'm so thirsty, though. I don't have money for drinks. What the hell am I doing. They're selling lemon ices on the corner and they're $2.50. I want one so bad I almost go into a panic.

I flash on *him* and my heart lifts into my throat again. I need him. I can feel him. I walk faster and then I'm full out running in my sister's punky shoes, sweat sliding down my back. The scene I've been replaying in my head comes back in macro vision. I can feel him grabbing the belt loops of my jeans, the shock of that, pulling me in, tight but not all the way, just close enough to make me look into his eyes. He made me want him so much.

Be there, be there.

When I get to the massive doors of Constellation, everything stops. I'm thirsty as if I'd been running for hours. No money for drinks.

And maybe he's not there.

I could turn back.

I could just walk the half mile back to Moon's right now.

If I went against every law of physics.

The place is dark and moody and now has the feeling of a nightclub. People are dressed so sparkly. Eyes electric, teeth shining, bare shoulder blades gleaming. Everyone belongs, like a thin, shining tribe. Some Italian techno opera is soaring through the air. Durgha flits by, head high. She is so short and tense, with the metallic red do and the high arched brows and tonight a small red tulip mouth. She catches my eye—no. I stand at the edge of the room, feeling like a twelve year old in a bar. I am looked at by many pairs of eyes, for just the briefest of moments, less than moments, passed over because there is nothing glam about me. Dumb dress, idiot aviator sandals, sticky folded paper ice in my hand. What, honestly, was I thinking?

But there he is.

Bending to kiss the carved cheekbone of a model at a crowded tiny table near the bar. He looks at me and his eyes do not cut away immediately. He smiles. I hold his gaze and my smile happens hugely, breaking straight out of my heart, as if I am Pippi Longstocking, returned from her sea voyage, strong as a horse, brave as a pirate. One more kiss to another cheek and he straightens, walks right to me. They're watching me now, everyone at the table, Durgha across the room, people by the potted plants. They look away, they whisper, he comes to me.

He stands before me, same height. And he looks like a

stranger. In the dim light his eyes are darker, unreadable. The beginnings of a beard on his face. He seems older, a little scary. Even though my heart rushes up in my chest to greet him. Even though I recognize all of it in his eyes and know he recognizes me, too. It doesn't matter that his face looks foreign; I have spent more time with his mind. The skin is a soul sack.

"Hello," he says. "Are you meeting someone? Do you need a table?"

Doubt floods in so fully I almost lose my balance. I think of every bad thing: the one dollar I have. That I'm not meeting anyone. That I am crazy. That I look so stupid and tall and young. He is a polite and mild superstar and I imagined everything. I just need to get out now, I just need to run and—

Stand still. Be here. Like an infant, I want my sister. I look around the room for some kind of anchor—a slice of sky through the open door to the roof. I look down at my hands—still scrawled with notes. He pretends to read my hand. Then catches my gaze. "Oh, I see you have a reservation," he says. Then he's Mr. Host again. Welcoming smile, eager to help. "So, a table for you?"

"I came to see you," I say quietly. My heart fills my ears.

He blinks, the smile fades, he takes a step back, but still his eyes are on mine. I have one second to establish that I am not a crazed psycho stalker fan. I am a spy who needs to give the password, to say or do something that will allow us to finally begin. The possibilities clog my mind—the Gauguin, the little boy in the pen, chasing the phantom mouse, the meeting in the maze.

What can you say when you have been summoned, except—"I'm—just here." The admission breaks something inside me with a jagged snap. Something has kicked me in the back of the knees and my face floods with blood. He catches me with his compassionate eyes. I cover my burning face with my hand, pull back, murmur an apology. He touches my shoulder, holds me in a quick, consoling hug. "It's okay," he says. "I understand; it's good you came."

It happens so quickly. The heat leaves my face. He leads me into the thick of the room. He seats me at a table with others. I look at my hands until he returns with a tall cranberry soda. "I remember," he says. "Anooshka."

I just nod. He said my name so casually and gently. Did he really say it?

The people at the table are pretending to not notice me. One of them is a tall girl chewing on one of those long, carved toothpicks that are supposed to help you quit smoking. A man with a small silver stick through his nose is playfully running an ice cube along the side of her neck.

Orpheus pulls a chair up and leans in close. "You know

that a lot of people are looking at us now. You understand that, don't you?"

I nod.

"I mean, if we want to hang out, we have to be subtle."

Not sure where this is going but anything, anything.

"Let's spend some time together tonight, would that be okay?"

I barely nod. He has such a gentle voice.

"I have to get away sometimes." He looks down for a beat and keeps talking, quickly, as if chatting with himself. "You came for a reason. It's going to be good. Just trust me." He looks into my face. "Can you do that? It's not easy for me to get away, but not impossible, either." Touches my cheek lightly. I am staring. "I know it's a huge leap, but just for a few more minutes, hang in, okay?"

Durgha is at the corner of the bar, now in a platinum wig and backless mini cut so low I can see butt cleavage. She's with two guys and a girl and she is talking to them, nodding, laughing. She keeps turning over her shoulder to check me out. I sip my drink and my whole face feels numb. I feel like I am on a drug and for a moment wonder if something has been put in my drink. But no, it's just panic.

I need to see my face. Sometimes you just have to look into your own eyes to know you're still there. Plus you might need a little more rosewood lipstick. The bathroom is like a sushi bar—all chrome and minimalist polished wood and a tall ivory candle burning. My face in the perfect subdued light in the perfect smoky mirror is okay. I am a brown-haired, brown-eyed girl with a rosewood mouth and natural white teeth and a smeared avocado stain on my corny denim skirt which I start attacking with a wet paper towel, pausing to check my teeth again in case they are green, and coming in now and standing next to me at the sink, watching me give myself the frozen wolfsmile, is Scarlett. A hot alarm goes off inside me. She's got some connection with *him*. She's wearing what looks like a black bandage wrapped around her breasts and ultra-short gauzy black shorts. Her hair's pulled back severely in a black headband and her eyebrows look as if they were painted with a skinny Japanese ink brush. "Hi, hon," she says, bored and casual.

"What are you doing here?"

"I live here. " She takes in the damp towel in my hand, the splotch on my skirt, with a kind of faint horror.

"In this building?"

Her answer is to breathe out heavily through her nose, curl half her mouth. So she means she lives in the city. Or she spends so much time at Constellation she practically lives here. Oh, who knows, who knows the thrilling mysteries that girls like Scarlett live.

"So you're sitting with your boyfriend, huh?" she says.

"I guess he's not gay after all."

"What?" For a minute I think she's talking about Raphael. I associate Scarlett with parties at Lindsay's. Seeing her out of context makes me feel even more cognitively impaired. And she won't let go of this Orpheus thing.

"Durgha's never seen you before."

So she knows Durgha. I feel like I'm at a cranked-up version of the scene at Lindsay's place. Same crew, same us-and-them feelings, same dramarama. Only instead of some rich druggie boy there's his antithesis, the soft, sweet Orpheus, who just happens to be a star.

Scarlett takes her long, breakable-looking legs back to the bar to report to Durgha. I spot Orpheus out on the roof, talking to some people. A guy from the hotel party wearing baby blue sunglasses (just like the ones Moon gave me!) comes to our table and perches on the edge of a girl's chair. He's all light and charming with a British accent. He leans in to me and says: "Hey morning glory. You are an innocent angel, aren't you?"

How could anyone answer such a thing. Yes, I am. No, I'm a faux king ho.

The guy has an expensive smell. I am dizzy from all the fame and stardom and sheen and gloss in this room. Cameras clicking. So many tiny digital poppings and framings. Little drinks. Shared huge plates of pixilated food.

Eyeshadow in those gradient, barely there hues that had to be applied by expensive geniuses. Pruned hair. Thin designer clothes made of bright ribbons and silver threads. Looks and preenings. This is not me or this is so me. How could I know without someone like ZZ Moon or Raphael to be here and see me and tell me how amazing it is. I can just see Marley and his flat eyes singing me the OCD song. Poof, be gone, focus, focus.

"Orpheus wants me to take you down to the corner and meet him in a few minutes, you up for that?" The guy says it all smooth and soft, and it all sounds like a terrible lie. This is where I go off and am not seen again. Even Scarlett and Durgha have disappeared from the bar. *There were no witnesses to her disappearance. I last saw her in the bathroom. I last saw her at a table, wringing her ink-stained paws.* This is the moment I have been warned about by third-grade teachers and my big sister. I could say no. Everyone is suddenly so old and beyond me. Someday I could be lying in a fragrant garden laughing about this. I could be sitting in Marie Henry's basil patch. But now things are sinister, the night is hot, and the music is so loud, and Orpheus is looking at me through the crowds, through his big rectangle glasses, nodding that it's cool to leave with this guy.

Take a leap.

Are you okay, love? says the man in the London accent

in the elevator going down.

Sure. Are you?

He laughs. I laugh.

He only asked because when I am so shy and scared I get that look of being on crack. I hate when near strangers ask are you okay. It's almost as bad as *smile*. How do they know you have not lost a grandmother or just learned about a child being mutilated somewhere? Moon taught me to say *"Are you?"* right back to them, in an equally concerned tone. It is among the ten best pieces of practical knowledge anyone has ever taught me.

The night heat hits our faces thick as Vaseline. The sky has the same orange-brown glow of what I remember from my one trip to Los Angeles to visit my father. Everyone is on the street, half nude, half drunk, and loud, or maybe sounds just sit heavier in the heated air. The London man steers me across the street to the little deli where Moon and I followed an ancient guy fifty years ago, thinking it was Orpheus. The deli has a new life inside. A glitter glam boy with pink lipstick and false eyelashes is elaborately stretching and bending over the counter to grab a pack of cigarettes.

"Want something, honeydoodle?" London Man asks me. "Some water, some coffee, cigs, lottery tickets, anything?"

He's put five packs of ginseng gum on the counter and he keeps tilting his head to the window, keeping watch. I tell him no thanks, although I want a drink, like a shot of tequila or JD, for the first time since the beginning of the summer. Like really, really want one. My heart is still trapped at the base of my throat.

A cab pulls up. "Here we go now," says London Man. He opens the door and then I'm sitting alone in the backseat with Orpheus and the car moves on. The cab is air-conditioned.

I sneak a look: he's beaming at me full of fun and adventure. I almost relax, but there is dream fuzz in my brain, such a thick sense of unreality. Almost like the paranoia I felt when I once smoked hash. Your face a giant balloon with a Magic Marker grin drawn on, looming out from your stringy neck.

He grabs my hand and examines it. "So you've got a book written here?"

He shows me his. I hold it. I'm touching Orpheus's hand. Is there a neutral feeling here, like me and Raphael? No. Is there a spark. Maybe, but he is twenty-one years *old* and he's a nerd. Maybe he's a nerd. But he's famous. But I love his music. He scares me. His hand, in my hand, is wide and beautiful with long fingers and large, rounded fingernails. On his hand: Patty and Johann, 8 p.m. Starling. Ochre.

"It's like appointment book meets lyric," I say. Did I say that?

"I like you," he says.

I almost say thanks, but better to say nothing.

Where could we be going? I wonder if he is going to try and sleep with me. I wonder if I would. Am I a groupie? In five years we will be practically the same age but now—

"Hey, Anooshka?" He touches my shoulder. "We're going to have a sweet time together. I could get you into trouble as fast as I could get you out of it, but—I'm not going to be any trouble to you at all."

"Good," I say.

He laughs. "Yeah, I'm glad to be with you. This is just what I needed. I'm starting to feel human again."

Then we are walking. On a long path by the Hudson, past creaky piers and lighted boats in the black, shiny river. An odd wind has come up, hot as the air from a subway grate.

With a baseball hat on his head and his glasses tucked in his pocket, he doesn't look like Orpheus.

We can walk for hours and no one will bother us, he says. He is so normal. Thin, normal jeans, normal sneakers, a black T-shirt with a white Japanese cartoon cat. He reminds me of Mr. Bono, a cool math teacher I had in the eighth grade. He had a lot of nervous energy and made us laugh. He'd been a rock drummer in high school and was always drumming on surfaces while we were trying to take tests, then catching himself and apologizing profusely. He had just graduated from college and gotten married to his high school girlfriend and he always talked about his wife. Once a year he would perform in the teacher's talent show and he would dance and lip-synch and the girls would scream because his moves were way hot. But on normal school days he was a normal man.

I am walking late at night with a famous twenty-one-year-old stranger who also feels as familiar as someone I've known since preschool. I am walking with the one I had a transcendent dialogue with.

"It's not just about our painted hands," he says, grabbing my hand again and holding both of our hands up to the muddy sky. "There are so many people, so many thought streams. People communicate in different ways, all the time . . . when you're sleeping, when you see a stranger on the subway . . . people are always psychically tapping you on the shoulder, but you don't have to answer."

"I guess people are always thinking they have some amazing connection to you," I say. "Because you're so available—with your diaries, your songs . . ."

"Yup," he says. "It's like living your whole life on a stage. I wanted it, but I don't want it. I want both, you know? I'm so insecure I want *that* guy to stop everything and recognize me, you know?"

He's talking about a guy way out on a boat docked at the end of the pier, messing around with a sail rigging.

"Even I want that," I say. "I want that guy to stop everything and notice me."

He stares at me and laughs. "You are so—present, or something."

"I'm just not an idiot in the usual way," I say.

"One thing it's not about is quick repartee." He looks at me. "Thank God we don't have that," he says.

"Yeah," I say. "I don't know how people do that. All those popular media references back and forth. This movie, that thing; I can't do that."

"Me either," he says. "I'm so slow."

I want to tell him about the Gauguin thing, how amazing it was that we both fixed on the same painting in the same way—but it suddenly seems like one of those media references.

"Do you think it's chemistry then?" I say. We stop at a bench that looks too decrepit to sit on so I just put my gladiator-laced foot up on it. The idea that something might happen, that we're out here on this hot summer night, that we might kiss—it frightens me. His face, so unexpectedly vulnerable, is even more foreign to me. There are things that seem too real and unexpected about his face—a normalness to his teeth, a smallness to his nose. A reddishness to the slight shadow of stubble on his chin, a thinness to his upper lip. His arms, with their tight muscles, have a sheen of perspiration. I focus in on the scar next to his eye because it makes him seem familiar somehow. But he's not even looking at me. There is no romance in the air. We're like two guy friends trying to remember what the hell ever did bring us together back there in the old days of Brooklyn or Berkeley or whatever.

"My parents had chemistry," he says. "They did it their first night together, and I popped out nine months later. And before I was two, she was screaming at him constantly. My first memory was her telling him how hard to put his foot on the gas. I was in the backseat with my fingers in my ears."

"So they got a divorce, huh?"

"Nah, they're still together. He screws around and drinks and she's a fuckin' shrew."

"I don't think people should talk to each other like that. No one should be a boss to another person."

He finally looks at me, cocking his head. "You don't, huh? Then you probably won't last in a relationship past six months—"

I start to protest—

"—which is a shame, because you'd probably make a great boss. You'd be a kind, dignified boss. . . ."

I laugh, and he brightens at the appreciation.

He perches with his skinny butt on the back of the bench and looks out to the dark waters. "No, it's not about bestial attraction," he says. "All the lust in the world—it means nothing. All the fun in the world, even that means nothing."

"Then what is it?"

"It's two things," he says. The black water's smacking against the piers with regular little *slap-slap-slap*s. I watch the infinitesimal waverings of a reflection cast by a docked boat. "It's about purpose," says Orpheus. "About always coming back to being kind to another being instead of trying to get something from them. But I try to do that with everyone."

"You do?"

"Yes, Saint Orpheus here. I know I sound so nerdy."

"No—"

"But I am a nerd. I kinda wish I was a normal rock star, driving around doing blow in the back of a limo—but I can't be that."

I start pacing a little in front of the bench, so he hops off his perch and we keep walking.

"So if you're nice to everyone—," I start, "or if you try to be kind to everyone, what's the other thing? What's the thing that makes for a special relationship?"

He stops to admire a huge tree arching over our path. He pats it fondly like it's an elephant trunk. He leans up against the tree, facing me. I feel so awkward. That animal thing rising up just because of the look in his eyes and the deep way he's looking at me.

"I think it's a sense of your mind resting with another's . . . do you know what I mean?" He looks at me so—intensely—something spirals in my stomach. That hot, strong wind comes off the river now and bits of paper and grit blow up around us. My hair whips into my eyes. He reaches out and grabs a handful. "Your hair is so dark," he says. He holds it between his fingers like silk, letting his fingers slide slowly down. "I love dark hair."

I feel pulled in and at the same time frozen. We're standing inches apart and the energy between us is dense and magnetic. He has a scent that is religious and nautical, like the sea, like the serene candle burning in the bathroom at Constellation. It stirs me, draws me in, draws me in.

"I'm not going to be your lover," he says. "That much we know."

"We do?" My voice is a whisper. His hand rests on the back of my neck and I want it there.

"I knew you were coming, though," he says. "I love that we recognize each other."

That he said it—it feels like a piece of a vast, scattered, complex, hopeless puzzle abruptly locking into place. Such relief.

"You recognize me, don't you?" His voice is so soft. With the lightest touch, his fingers run down my neck and all the way down my arm. He takes my hand in both of his. "Do you?"

"Of course," I say.

The ambiguities are making me feel like my head is floating off my body. He says we are not going to be lovers and he touches me like we already are. I feel like he might be more than a soul mate, we might be something bigger— but it's scary, too—

Maybe he's a cult leader with lots of little me's locked up underneath some suburban mall somewhere. And each night we all hold up our hands and they're all written on and we all have brown eyes and bright smiles and we all just turned sixteen and we were all mesmerized by the same Gauguin painting which we all went to see because the subliminal messages in his diary sent us there. . . .

"Don't worry, I'm not clinically insane." He's laughing at me. "You were thinking that, right? Come on, you were."

"A little."

"Just a little psychotic, huh?" He lets go of my hand and we walk, a yard apart, and the buddy feeling is there again. The tendons in the back of my knees are suddenly made out of rubber. I look at him, but he's in his own happy arena again, looking into the distance. I feel confused.

Relieved. Sad. Touch me again. Grab me. Leave me alone. Shock at my own momentary paranoia. We walk. I'm starving. He asks if I'm hungry. My appetite flees.

21. We

From the crowd to the shore / from look to look /
. . . .
to follow his views—his breaths—his day

—from "Genie," Orpheus Sample of the New Directions Classic
by Arthur Rimbaud (Louise Varese, translator), © New Directions

It's hardly intimate! The dim sum joint is brightly lit and
noisy with the constant rising and falling of Chinese, spiked
with the sharp hiss and scrapings from the open kitchen.

The air-conditioning is ice. I pour two packets of sugar
into a small, steamy cup of tea. I look at him over the little blue cup and feel like I'm in a music video, playing his
girlfriend. The camera tilts at crazy angles, swooping
through the crowd of eaters, taking in the smoke and noise,
settling at last on my scrawled-on hand raising the cup to
my mouth. Orpheus is gazing at me with the calmest face.
I begin to relax.

"I recognized you when I first saw you," he tells me.

I feel a spasm of happy dread.

"I could see that you were grave and beautiful and

were a certain kind of soul."

"What kind?" I have no appetite for all the colorful dishes looming up from the giant stiff plastic menu. Bowls of cheerful pink organs, spiky anemones, green confetti of seaweed.

Orpheus runs two fingers down my arm, lightly, to bring back my attention. He smiles and puts his glasses back on and his eyes seem even kinder. "When you're in the city, and you're walking down the street through a sea of people," he says, "it's so amazing that sometimes not one of them looks at you or if they do, they usually look through you. Or quickly away. Or worse—if they hold your eyes it's for some perverse grasping lonely desperate impulse . . . but you just looked at me and saw me."

I have to tell Orpheus about that singing Buddhist monk who shows up sometimes at my school in his saffron and burgundy robes. He's the head of the monastery down the road and decided a few years ago to let his teenage girls attend public school rather than be cloistered away. I tell Orpheus how the guy always goes to the school concerts and I see him in the halls during the intermission. Parents and relatives of the kids pack the hallways and make me feel dizzy with their buzzing thoughts, and I look at their faces and no one really looks back. "Not even the parents of kids I've known for years," I tell Orpheus. "But that Buddhist father, he's aware of things. He always smiles right into you."

"But you saw him, Anooshka, get it?" Orpheus leans forward with eagerness. "That's what you're like. I could spot you in a room of a thousand because you would see me seeing you."

He orders a tray of tiny delicacies with spicy little red and green sauces swimming with chili seeds and pink peppercorns. I take one bite, three. Can barely eat. He is starving and finishes everything.

"What's wrong?" he says. "Why can't you eat?"

I tell him that I'm just not hungry.

"All the nourishment can now come from the beloved," he says in a vampire voice. "Yes, a feeling as ancient as the infant brain. Ah, Mother, now I can eat at last! Feast, nurse at the neck of the beloved. . . ."

I must look freaked because he leans over and ruffles my hair. "Don't worry, Anooshka, I'm playin' wid chew, girrrl." He sips his tea. "I should maybe be telling you that you can't trust a man like me, but you can."

He's right—but trust him to do or not do what?

It's four A.M. and we're on the roof of Constellation. The heat has either faded a few notches or we have just grown used to the hot darkness. There are no stars to see. No one is here. Everything has been cleaned and put away. It's quiet.

He stands behind me at the roof's edge, looking over my shoulder into a telescope, swinging it this way and that until he gets what he wants. "Ah! There! Now don't move it—look right where I have it."

A blue cartoon character with bugging-out eyes. Some man's watching TV. He turns the scope again and I see a woman gazing out the window. She has sculpted hair like a pampered pooch. Orpheus turns it again and all I see is the muddy haze of sky.

"I don't see anything—" His face is close.

"I know," he says, into my ear. I lose my breath. His scent is more complicated than before. Damp sand, a strip of green tree bark, black pepper. None of those! His hand on the back of my neck. I'm in a panic, more fear than lust, and then in the center of my screaming heart comes a soft kiss on my cheek.

"That's all," he says. "I just wanted to do that. Is that okay?"

I nod. Relief and disappointment as he pulls back.

"Let's go," he says. "If you're not bored yet . . ."

I follow him like a brave kitten. That would be okay if someone were to say that about me in a third-person narrative—but in my own reality, it feels like a weak and soft thing to be. I'm like someone who has feared an accident at a specific moment in time and now that the time has passed feels a relief—but also a letdown. My chemistry has been altered by finally being with him. My brain has squeezed out the last drop of the thing that drives me and now I am beginning to move in reverse.

His loft is just around the corner. He lets us in through a series of locked doors and then we take an elevator to the top floor. The place is surprisingly stark. Everything is shut away behind tall blond cabinets. Butterscotch wooden floors with a few lush carpets scattered about. Wide glass doors open onto a balcony filled with potted trees and a city view, taking up a whole side wall. There's a lingering smell of cedar incense. Tall, pale pink candles everywhere. A giant comfy couch faces a black metal fireplace. A bunch of his music awards are casually arranged on the mantel.

Orpheus calls to me from the kitchenette off the living room, through the sounds of a machine clanking ice into glasses. "I'm making you some iced tea."

In the corner is a long, beaten-up desk with an open laptop. I wander over to the desk and check out the hundreds of cards and photos pinned onto a cork board. I scan it, ridiculously looking for familiar faces—and there they are. Or there *she* is. Durgha is the star of many photos. Standing in a snowsuit making a snowman on the roof of Constellation; snapped underwater among tropical fish; always with a big smile, just for Orpheus. They are together in photos, not looking like lovers, and she is alone in many pictures, just like lovers are photographed alone, by the other lover.

Orpheus appears with the drink and I gulp it. "Slow down, pardner," he says, laughing. "There's plenny mo' where that came from."

We both stare at the photos.

"I'm trying to see what you're seeing," he says. "They look sorta lame, from someone else's perspective. Or at least ordinary."

"Are you in love with Durgha?" I blurt.

He doesn't laugh. "Oh no," he says. "Durgha and I are like drinking buddies without the drinking."

"I thought she might have been the one you were writing about in your diary—about obsession. . . ." I look away from him, out at the shining view.

"Uh, no." He touches my chin, turning me gently back to him. He looks at me for two beats, and it seems like he's going to tell me something deep—and then says: "Hey, wanna hear some music?"

His music room is small and windowless but cooler than the rest of the loft, a relief to be in. I unlace those crazy sandals of Moon's and my feet sink into the lush raspberry-colored carpet. "Just get comfy with those if you want." I lie back against the huge silk pillows. He sits down at a computer, which is attached to a keyboard and a ton of sound equipment. I see an old blues record and a stack of forty-fives from the sixties.

"I'm working on this new thing," he tells me. "It's pretty amazing. Yeah, I know, egomaniac of the worst type. But it has so little to do with me. I just cook it all up, put a pause in here, slow this song down, speed this one up, and cut it in half. It's more like kitchen science. Or designing a building." He types in a code and the screen comes to life with something that looks like a heart monitor—all levels and mathematical codes.

I scan the spines of a few books on a shelf at my eye level. Sartre's *Nausea*! I pluck it out of the shelf, start thumbing through it excitedly.

"Are you bored already?" Orpheus peers at me over the controls.

"No—" I debate telling him that I imagined him reading this book in his hotel room. Better not to sound psycho. Slip the book back and close my eyes.

A crackly hiss comes out of the speakers and then this warm, slow voice that's barely human. Old female blues singer. And then a new voice, Orpheus singing an extravagantly slowed version of a seventies hit. The two voices overlap, pull apart, take turns.

He clicks at this, clicks at that, and then focuses on me. "You do want to hear this?"

All I can do is nod.

"You look sad," he says. He's staring at me as the music unfolds.

"It's just how I look sometimes," I tell him.

Dark cellos, bright piano, and the squeezed-out sounds of gypsy accordions tie two lonely voices together, tracing around them in wide circles and soft ropes of sound. Low, constant drums and organ chords rumble underneath. It's an eerie effect, like the world has paused and the only life is in these two people, singing their separate songs, taking turns calling to each other from different time zones, in different languages.

Our eyes meet and he looks at me so long, it seems as if he'll say something, but he turns back to the monitor.

He adds a new track, an Orpheus sample of an ancient French surrealist poem by Rimbaud, uttered in his rumbly voice, almost a monotone, a percussive instrument beneath the waves of melody and song: "*. . . in a dense breeze, constantly moving about but unable to elude the fabulous phantoms of the heights where they were to have met again . . .*"

Orpheus listens deeply, watching the levels rise and fall on the monitor, rocking slightly in his swivel chair. He's a nice guy, I think. He's like a nice guy on the beach watching the waves. I feel at peace, no trace of that crazy need to find him. The peace is just a thin shell, though; beneath it I can still feel that immense sense of longing. How insane to long for someone who is right in the room. It's late, almost morning. I close my eyes to feel the music inside.

The song winds down with slidey, shimmery guitar and slow cymbals, and works on me like a lullaby or drug. It's short and ends suddenly, on the intake of a breath.

"Can I hear it again?" I say.

"You can hear it as many times as you want," he says. "I can never live with anyone because I play stuff so many times it becomes like a torture. I just have to do that sometimes." He presses a button and the song will keep playing as our own soundtrack for the rest of the night and into the morning, beginning each time with that warm hiss and crackle and ending each time with the suddenness of a sob.

When we emerge from the cool room, the sky outside is a paler shade of orange murk. "I'm making you a bubble bath," Orpheus tells me. The singer sings on, her voice like organ chords. The bath runs. "It's going to take a while," he tells me. "The pressure here is nonexistent."

We sit outside in the almost sunrise, nestled into a gently swinging, freestanding hammock. White blossoms of jasmine send out their lemony honey scent. Shoots of feathery bamboo make it feel like Gauguin land. My hand rests in his hand, my body feels weightless and relaxed, as if we are floating off this balcony into the muggy air, in this pale orange time between night and day.

I tell him now about the Gauguin painting and how I

screamed when I read his diary and realized he'd seen the same painting and had the same thoughts.

"Anooshka . . ." He squeezes my hand. "What are we going to do?"

I shake my head. I hear a bird starting up. The sky is getting lighter.

"You know Orpheus and Eurydice are really just Adam and Eve," he says.

"No, I didn't know that," I say in a teasing voice.

His hand flies to his face, embarrassed. "God, I'm sorry. Sometimes I sound like some kind of dork professor."

"No, tell me about them." I want his hand back. It doesn't come back, though, and I look into his eyes in the new morning light; he's so strange, and so familiar, a dear alien. I already feel a wave of love for him.

"Well, just that they were perfect together—and then the snake came—and really, if someone had just said put that anaconda back in its cage, for chrissake."

"What do you mean?"

"Sex. It ruined everything. That's why—" He looks away.

I touch his arm. "What? That's why what?"

He looks back, grips my arms, pulls me closer, so close my heart squeezes. Strokes my cheek, looks into my eyes, smells like a dark forest. Whispers: "That's why I will never fuck you."

In the deep bath, hidden by silky bubbles. I feel the oddness of being naked in a man's house, but the door is locked. I feel safe, not exposed, okay except for a knotty ache gathering behind my eyes. I look at my reflection in the window that takes up a wall of the bathroom. My face is transparent; behind it are the scattered lights of the city, and the lights make me think of the people just getting up for work and the people who never went to bed. A thrill of early morning excitement runs through me; none of those people could possibly be as ecstatic as me. None of them have heard such a call to find someone and then found themselves soaking happily in his tub as if life were just an easy dream. I flash on random details from his diary—the cilantro chips he ate, the pattern of the hotel carpet, his feelings about the strangers he met and the portraits of his friends—and realize that he drew me in like a juicy book. I'm here inside his book now, in this herb- and lavender-scented tub, buried beneath bubbles, drifting. The headache blurs, disappears. The song plays on, the singer's melancholy voice melting my edges. Now Orpheus's voice, way slowed down, coming in and making my face heat up, warmth spread on my eyelids, like sun on a beach, gentle rays of his voice, bathing my face, my neck—hey—

It is the sun. I look for my face in the window and it's gone. Instead the city glows with fresh morning light, the sky a delicate turquoise and the sun hot on my face.

"Are you awake in there?" He's knocking. "I have tea for you when you come out. And you can borrow some pj's from the shelf."

I feel shaky from not sleeping. I look in the mirror over the sink and see I still have remnants of lipstick on and suddenly I want more. Lipstick addict. I have a flash of being trapped here, a prisoner given bubble baths and delicacies, never to be seen again. I think of Moon and also Ma—both sleeping at this time in the morning. I think of the puppy. He's always ready for a walk. If I were back home I'd be sneaking down the stairs and I would hear his *thump thump* of a tail and we'd be out in the daybreak walking by the muddy river. Such weird thoughts. Glad I'm here. The song still goes on. Maybe there's a subliminal message. *Where they were to have met again . . .*

I take some toothpaste—it's the fennel-flavored kind from the health food store—and squeeze some on my finger and rinse it around in my mouth with water from the tap. I pick a pair of striped pj's from a stack and wonder if some girl has been here before me, doing the same thing. Maybe a girl every night, or maybe just Durgha. I put on my own stained clothes and slump down on the bathroom floor. I can't come out in my dirty clothes. Take them off, put his pajamas on, just like the ones I pictured him wearing when he was alone in the hotel room. I don't want my sweet dream to turn nasty. Back in your cage, I tell the anaconda.

"Wait, I have to tell you about that time in the London Zoo. . . ." We have talked for the past six or seven hours, but we keep telling stories. We're in bed together, somehow. It's a huge bed, bigger than king sized. There's a yard of space between us as we sit up against pillows gazing in the general direction of a flat screen TV flickering with a cartoon featuring an orange dog. The sound is off and we can still hear the song, not loud but clearer than ever, coming through the tiny speakers at his ceiling. The bed is low and the floor is covered with green tatami mats. We each have trays by our sides of the bed—mine with a pitcher of French chocolate milk and a silver bowl of whipped cream, his with strong tea and toast and jam. Orpheus is cheerfully awake. Not me. I can hardly follow his story about the zoo, and can't even remember if he told it to me earlier. The blinds are closed tight and the room is dark and chill. Tall, pink candles flicker on low tables.

I feel clean and light. It was easy and natural to climb into the bed, no sense of the sexual. But now that I am here I have that feeling I get on airplanes the instant the plane is aloft; I'm so light-headed, I want to sleep. I never can sleep on planes, although sometimes I close my eyes and dream images start flickering beneath my lids while I'm still awake to watch. There's something about the atmosphere in Orpheus's bedroom that puts me in that exact state. I can't keep my eyes open and even though we are talking, I start to drift. . . .

He takes my hand. "Are you all right, sleepyhead?"

"Just drowsy," I murmur. He comes closer, leans over me. I feel him looking at my face. "Beautiful Anooshka," he says quietly.

I see wings.

"You're dreaming, aren't you?" My eyes, heavy as mountains, open for a second and see his peaceful gaze, looking at me fondly as a mother. "What are you seeing?" he asks gently. It's like being on the absolute verge of going under anesthesia, with Orpheus the gentle nurse, recipient of all my random secrets.

"My bird—" is all I can say.

"What, my darling, your bird?" I can feel his hand tighten with concern.

. . . every leaf on every tree in crisp relief, the shadows and patches of sunlight sharp as life. I'm searching the tree-tops in Central Park. That same sense of panic as when Zack flew off and I had the revelation that trees are immensely high and the world is so full of them and a tiny bird can easily be lost.

My eyes fly open and he passes his hand smoothly over my face, closing my eyes. "What a bad dream," he says, making little *shush, shush*ing sounds as if to calm me out of the nightmare.

Dream

He pulls me to him and there, in his arms, I fall deeply asleep and dream. When I wake, I'm on my side, and he's pressed up behind me, arms tight around me, kissing my cheek. The dream was so vivid it makes my heart race. I'm already gathering the fragments as I feel his body and take in the room, with the surreal blending of the candles and the morning light. The dream lands back inside me with a thud.

"You were sleeping so deeply," Orpheus says into my neck. I feel things stirring inside me—but he pulls away and gives me space; I roll over and stare at him. He's propped up on his elbow. His face looks tired. There's a shadow on his chin. He looks older in this light. And then I remember the end of the dream—so sickening . . .

"What did you dream?" he asks.

I look away—this is really impossible, immensely

embarrassing, to be here with him, to have dreamed in front of him. "It was so long—"

"I have time. . . ."

"Besides, I woke up—because someone was kissing my cheek—"

"Just one kiss," he says, like a scolded kid. "A very chaste kiss. I had nothing to do while you were snoring away."

"Hey!"

"I happen to find snoring a sexy thing. But—you need an ending to that dream—a happy one."

"You tell it," I say.

"No, you have to start," he says. "The dreamer gets first crack."

"Okay," I say, closing my eyes and making it up as I go:

"You and I are jumping off the top of a tree. My bird is with us and we fly gently down to the ground. The air is fresh and sweet, and you and I are like children, special friends, we have something higher than the physical. . . ."

"That's good," Orpheus says, with excruciating softness into my ear. "That's beautiful. But that's not gonna happen."

And I open my eyes, because he's pulling me close to him, his hands at the back of my neck, his mouth soft and salty against mine, just briefly, the softest kiss. And I'm nestled into him now, looking up at him.

"Just give me something," he says. "Now that I've awakened you." He pulls my hand to his mouth, and I'm happily shocked to see it is still written on, stars and numbers and words and pictures. "Give me one of these," he says, kissing one of my fingers. Or this one. Or this one. Or this—"

And now he kisses my mouth again, a real kiss, as he presses against me, and I feel deep swirls inside, screams, wanting, my heart slamming—

"But you said—"

"For a visual person, you put so much emphasis on words—," he says gently. Another slow, soft kiss. "Just be with me now."

Just when I would have done anything and it was too late to stop because just his warmth against me and his mouth on my neck makes me writhe inside—just then he pulls away and props up on his elbow and says:

"But it's not a bad thing to believe in words, and you really should be able to trust what I say."

I beat my fists into the bed and growl at the ceiling.

"Are you growling?" he says, peering into my face. How can he be so calm?

"Sadist!" I grab the neck of his shirt and pull him on top of me. "Stop talking," I tell him.

"Okay," he says, tugging at my pajama pants and slipping them off so smoothly. He pulls me tight and close and there's the shock and intense pleasure of our bare skin touching. A vast and fragile silence. And then he moves inside me, rocking so slowly against me.

"Anooshka, look at me," he says. And his eyes, so calm, make me wild.

After, I cry. Not right away. I go in his bathroom—by then it's almost afternoon—take a shower, and come out in a robe. The candles haven't burned out yet. I have the sense of keeping my face cheerful. He's still in bed and reaches his hand up for me.

"Oh, what's wrong?" he says. "You have that sad look again. I thought I might make it go away forever; you look like—you look like you have so much pain inside—oh, just come here."

He makes a tent of the sheets and I crawl in with him, in the robe, hair dripping wet. We talk in the tent.

"I feel you're keeping yourself from crying, that it's this close to your surface. Just breathe, honey, and let it all out."

I do it. One breath, two, and something becomes unstuck. I cry for a while, and he holds me and passes me tissues.

After, we come out for air and lie there looking at each other.

He has such a good face. Some people's faces get demented when you look at them too long, but his only gets better.

"You're not crazy," he tells me. "Your feelings are real."

"Everyone always thinks it's real, even when it has nothing to do with love," I say. "Even when it's just a sickness."

"Oh," he says, "you mean most of the people in the world."

Right, I guess.

"It takes time to know someone." He's touching my mouth with a velvet fingertip. "Do you like what you know so far?"

I grab his hand away. "You could be some rock star!"

"Yeah." He's amused.

"A player, you know, just saying things—"

"I could."

"That would be terrible."

"It would, yeah—but how would you know—how would you know if I was going to stick around or just be a bastard . . . how would you really know?"

"Maybe if we had breakfast together?"

He laughs his low rumble of a laugh. "Is that all it takes? Cool." He leaps up from the bed. "Waffles or eggs?"

"No! I'm not hungry!" I say. It'll take something else.

He's back in the bed. "What then? You tell me."

I don't know what to tell him; I'm just empty.

"Okay, I'll tell you." He seems unnaturally sane. It's so good to be with a man instead of a boy. But how can he be so alert and cheerful when I'm so wrung out?

He brushes a wet strand of hair off my cheek. "You're afraid that you're just running after a projection of your mind . . . and what you want is real love, right?"

I stare at the ceiling. The whole day is sliding by. Guilt. Emptiness. Can't believe he's so focused on me, caring this much.

"Don't be shy—that's what you want, right?"

"Yeah, I guess." I put his pillow over my head. He yanks it off and holds it over me with mock threat.

"No, that's what you want, damn it!"

"Okay then, boss!"

"Look, Anooshka, come here . . ." He opens his arms. "Come on." I just cuddle against his chest and let his words wash over me. "So if you have all these feelings and they don't seem particularly real and then I have all these feelings—"

A colored ribbon spirals inside me—he does have all these feelings?

"—and then we keep having them for each other, and it keeps going on, maybe even for a really long time, and we're kind to each other—then maybe there is no problem."

I slip out of his warm embrace and edge off the bed. "I'm a little overwhelmed," I say. "I think I'll just go sit on your balcony for a second."

"Right," he says. "I completely understand." And then he dives for me, pulling me onto the bed, making me squeal, all the weirdness lifting off my body like a bad hex.

"Now you're really going to get it," he says. He just barely touches his mouth to mine, and then again, and again with hunger, his hands in my hair, pulling me closer, language all gone.

22. My One and Only

*I can't hold you tighter but I'll find a way / outside it's
raining and nothing ever stays / nothing ever stays*

—from "Leaving," © ORPHEUS XTIIMUSIC

I'm lying on him in the cocoon of the slow-moving cab.
Our hands are tangled, fingers curled so easily together. The
day's turned moist, warm and gray, the heavy air coming
through the open windows. "I shall find you," he whisper-
sings, a purr in my ear. "I'll be at your feet." We both have
the exhilarated fatigue of people just arrived from another
country. The heat somehow muffles the outside sounds,
creating a cozy blur of horns, muted jackhammers, and
shouts in rapid languages. The whole city smells like
burned coffee. We both drift; I awaken with a careening
sensation, feeling him awakening too, his arms grabbing
me tighter as the cab comes to a halt. The driver says: "This
would appear to be it, folks."

We say good-bye outside of Moon's apartment, in the
sodden atmosphere, the light turning odd and greenish.
He'll be on a plane to London in four hours. We wrap our

arms around each other and our bodies just settle instantly into each other. My face against his clean, warm shirt, breathing him in, his beautiful smell making me dizzy. He's so familiar now, like the real man has caught up with my ethereal vision. He looks different—instead of the shy smile and the hesitant look in his eyes, his whole face is relaxed. His eyes have a new depth and he's looking at me fully, with more than fondness. He looks happy, that's what it is.

A gentle euphoria is part of the atmosphere, the air speaking of colors just beyond the visible spectrum. I close my eyes and we kiss and when I feel the tears wet my cheeks I'm so surprised. So it is true, I'm thinking, even as I'm tasting his kiss, you can cry tears of joy without even knowing you're crying. It's just like those things you read in books where the person hears a scream and then realizes it's her own. I never believed in that until now. But then there are way too many tears and I realize it's raining.

"I thought I was crying," Orpheus tells me.

Moon is all quiet and weird, staring at me when I let myself in. I didn't even expect her to be here. Her eyes are strange and small.

"Are you crying?" She's got her back to the sink, gripping the counter, as if it's holding her up.

I go to put my arms around her and she doesn't hug me back.

"Moon, what's wrong? Is it Ma?" I look at the phone for some reason. "Did something happen to Ma?" For the first time since Ma's call last night, I remember that I never called her back. Moon must've covered for me. "Did Ma find out I was gone last night? What is it? Are you pissed at me? I'm sorry, Moon, I—" The floating feeling inside me, the blurry happy sense of having him still with me—it seems big enough to obliterate any problem Moon's having.

She shakes her head, tearing up. "Is it Marley—did you break up?" Selfishly, I have a fleeting disappointment; I won't be able to go on and on about Orpheus if she's all upset about Marley.

"It's okay," I tell her.

"Take a breath, honey." She grips me hard by the arms and looks into my face. "It's Zack."

She doesn't want to tell me what happened, but I make her say all of it.

Ma got up early in the morning and opened the front door to take Taj out. *I was in Orpheus's bed then.* She remembered she'd left the kettle on and, with the door still open, she ran into the kitchen. *He was telling me to look at him.* She saw Taj running out the door with something in his mouth. *I was screaming.* She turned off the kettle. Went outside. Saw Taj on the front porch with Zack in his mouth. She got hysterical and took my baby out of his mouth. *I was holding on to him, moving.* She left my little darling on the porch and yelled at the dog and hit the dog and ran in the house to call Moon. She found poor Moon at Marley's, woke her up shrieking. *He was telling me I was perfect, so perfect.* Moon told her to go outside and see if Zack was alive, go outside and be with his body if he was dead. Ma went out and Zack was gone. That's when Moon started going crazy. *I was tossed in waves of pleasure.* She and Ma were on the phone both screaming. Ma never found him, but she was sure he was dead. She said a lot of his feathers were left behind on the porch. *I was in his bathroom crying.* He had been so wet when she took him out of Taj's mouth. He must have died of shock. Taj must have taken him and hidden him somewhere while Ma went back in the house. *Where was my connection then? Where was I?*

I find myself in the park in the afternoon, stunned. Everything has been washed with the brief rain and the grass is wet, steam rising from the paths, trees glistening. Birds everywhere. Each one cuts through my insides like a paper-thin knife. I lean against an ornate outdoor staircase leading down to a fountain in a courtyard. Three little brown birds hop along the wide sides of the staircase and they make me just choke up. If there weren't so many people around, I would throw myself on the ground and sob for hours. I'm afraid to be alone, though. The pain that's waiting is too big to deal with.

I look at the little birdies and pray to God, to anyone, to Zack. "Please give me a sign that you're near. Oh Zack, where are you?"

One of the birds flies off and leaves two. That cannot be a sign. Maybe Zack has met his mate in heaven. The two brown birds fly off. There is no sign, no sign, nothing. And then I see what I have been staring at this whole time—the entire ornate staircase is a carving of birds— hundreds of birds intertwined on branches. I know that's the sign, but those birds are frozen. I can smell Zack—his far-off scent of anisette, pepper, pirates—feel his slight weight on my finger, on the top of my head, see his intense gaze, his cocked head, hear his joyful singing. I long for the profound empathy that passed between us. Standing there crying, hugging myself, I wonder what would have hap- pened if Ma had died instead.

Bird 9,087 is gliding overhead, and I realize it's a plane. Orpheus is up there somewhere now, and my one and only thought about him is: he will never see Zack.

The next day Moon takes off work and we drive upstate in the hot Honda. While Ma's making preparations for a backyard funeral, Moon and I hang out in the kitchen looking for food. There's signs of Zack everywhere— droppings by his favorite perches, shed iridescent feathers here and there.

The puppy is out front in the fenced-in yard, crying,

whining, even howling because we're inside and he wants to see us.

"I feel sorry for him," says Moon, digging around for something in the bottom of the fridge. "He doesn't know what he did."

"Well, I hate him," I say. "I can't even look at him."

Moon stands, empty handed. "Nothing to eat—as usual."

"Yeah, Ma makes me sick."

"Anooshka!" She seldom takes this tone and it makes me jump. "Leave Ma alone; she loved Zack like crazy."

"No, she didn't!" Even though I know she did. "If she wasn't so damn obsessed with getting that freaking dog! She was on the Internet the whole summer!"

"Yeah? And you don't even realize you're just like her!"

This hits me like a smack in the mouth. "What are you talking about?"

"Oh, never mind!" Moon hates confrontation. She's pouring herself a glass of water and glugging it down. "Let's go help Ma."

We both peer out the kitchen window. Ma's dragged the stereo system outside and the beginning of a Beatles tune floats into the house. I see her on her knees in the garden, digging beneath the Japanese maple tree. It's a little sapling, only up to our knees, which she promises will someday give us shade and make the garden a classy place.

"We can go in a sec. What do you mean I'm like her?"

"Sweetie, you're just obsessed, that's all. You spent the whole summer online yourself. The Orpheus thing."

"But I'm with him now," I tell her. My voice comes out sounding like a defensive little kid. *But I'm big enough for that ride.* I hate her for that. I hate myself for hating her. I just break out crying.

"Honey!" She grabs me. "Oh, honey, I'm so sorry!"

"No, you're right, ZZ," I say into her chest. "Ma got her puppy; I probably won't even hear from him again."

"Sweetie, you will." Why is her voice the only thing that can soothe me? Why do I want to put her voice in a bottle and pour it straight into my heart at times like this? "I didn't mean anything by that. You're really not like Ma. Not much, anyway. Just more than me—and sometimes it makes me jealous. "

When it's time for the funeral, Ma's dead asleep in her room. In the middle of the afternoon! "She's depressed," says Moon. "She's depressed about Zack; don't wake her up. We'll have the funeral by ourselves."

This time I am going to kill Ma. This time she's not going to get away with her old selfish tiny cute woman tricks. "Get up!" I scream at her. "You're acting like a spoiled baby!" She's looking at me blearily, already trying to get out of bed. I'm hysterical, a feeling I've never had, an emotion that takes over your body and makes it move by itself. I'm grabbing a pillow and hitting her with it, Moon's screaming, grabbing me around the waist, pulling me. "Get the hell up," I'm telling the little woman. "You're not the baby—I'm the baby! Do you hear me? I'm the fucking baby!" I get on the floor and start howling, sixteen years of all of *it*, trying to get out, tasted in my throat, boiling up in my guts, screaming itself out.

Ma played the old song "Blackbird." *Blackbird singing in the dead of night.* Ma lit sage and Buddhist incense and wafted it around each of us. We all said prayers. We buried the green plastic bird that Zack had talked to since he was a baby, his inanimate, brain-dead mate for life. Maybe it would grow wings and a soul and fly off with Zack.

23. Love Is Chemical

That feeling you feel / doesn't mean it's real

—from "Take It Away," © ORPHEUS XTIIMUSIC

I wake every morning with the missing. I lie on my side and feel the missing—now sharp, now a weight, eating into that spot between the top of my stomach and the center of my chest. I don't want to talk to Orpheus; I want to feel his body. Relief would come with consolation, his chest pressed against the missing spot, his arms tight around me.

But to miss a bird—when he was alive, I couldn't hug Zack, but his voice flooded my heart. How impossible to love a being that you could not hug, to love it with all you had and to know you were so completely loved back by this being that could not hug you. And the connection remains when he dies, only deeper and more impossible.

Our most intimate contact came one day three years ago. I had the flu and couldn't get out of bed, and Ma, as she often did when I was sick, took to her own bed with phantom symptoms. Zack stayed on my head as I slept, guarding me, leaving only to get sustenance from his cage, eating hurriedly like a chicken, dipping his beak briefly in his water. I fell asleep on my back, propped on a pillow, my mouth half open, and woke suddenly in the twilight, puttering and spitting, with the sound of Zack's startled squawk and flap as he flew off my head—he had shit in my mouth!

I didn't miss that, of course, although we wouldn't be able to laugh at his silly tricks again. To miss Zack was to literally miss a song you would never hear again, your favorite song.

But where are you, I say to Orpheus, ten times a day, a thousand times a day. And the same cry to Zack, louder, because he was my shadow, always following me, flying, in and out of every room of my house.

A week after we had Zack's funeral, the longing was so great I went into the woods and did my special whistle for him. *Chit-choo, chit-choo.* No one answered, but the neighbor heard me and he told me that he'd found Zack's body on our lawn, weeks ago. The air was sucked out of me. The neighbor stood there with a faint smile on his face, standing with his hose, watering the red geraniums in his window box, as if this revelation was just a strange inconvenience—like the garbage not being picked up this week. The neighbor said he was so surprised that we'd just left the body there. "I picked it up." His referral to Zack as an *it* made my head feel as light as if it were going to float up off my shoulders. "It had become a mummy, really, in the heat. And I put it in a tree in your yard."

The neighbor was weird and I wanted to kill him, but the neighbor, like the puppy, did not know what he was doing or saying or the impact. I let him lead me to what was left of Zack and it was true: nothing of Zack in there. I read somewhere that when you see the corpse of your beloved you know the soul no longer resides there. So it was with Zack. There was nothing to it, like a piece of dried leather with half a dozen luminous pastel blue feathers, clean, resting among the thick foliage beneath. I put the feathers in a bag and mailed them to ZZ Moon, because she asked for them. I wrapped his body and buried it in the spot where his plastic friend had been buried, and said my own final good-bye.

"Look," Orpheus said to me, the morning we last saw each other, under the shelter of my sister's awning, as fat drops of rain smacked the pavement. "I can't stand leaving you now. Why don't you come with me?"

I laughed. "I could never do that."

I play back these scenes as if they will help me reconstruct reality. Orpheus must have seen the panic in my face when we were saying good-bye, because he said: "You don't have to worry about anything. Look at me." He tipped my chin up. "Really, this is not a normal thing that has happened between us. You know that."

I nod.

"Okay, then." He asked me for my e-mail and wrote it on his hand. I had a sense that I might never hear from him again. That the rain would wash it away. I wanted to ask him when he would write to me, and if I could have his e-mail too—but that early afternoon was painted with such ethereal joy that to ask such a practical thing would have been like Juliet asking Romeo if he could throw the wet clothes in the dryer. Orpheus said he'd find me, so I was sure he would.

The intensity of the moment was so great that it made me live only in my senses, breathing in the electric smell of the pavement, feeling his weight against me and the warmth of his last kiss. And my heart turned sad with hope the moment he turned his back.

I wake from an afternoon sleep so tired I feel as if I have salt in my blood. At work I almost quit because Marian's giving me such a hard time. First she said my hair looked like rats' tails. Now she's asking me if I'm on drugs because I forgot to do a setup for table six. Yeah, I just came from shooting up, dollface! I have to make another two hundred before summer's over, to buy an amazing silver bug that Ma's friend is promising me for only twelve hundred dollars. So quitting's out. I race into the kitchen with a load of filthy dishes when an Orpheus song starts to play. That killer one-minute song with the funky bass and the techno beat:

> *If this isn't real*
> *take it away take it away take it away*
> *that feeling you feel*
> *take it away take it away take it away*
> *doesn't mean it's real*

I haven't heard from him yet. The words of the song are beginning to take on new meaning.

One night Ma is normal. She is pretty and not crazy and she has a patience and tenderness about her that is reminiscent of my sister. I almost want to ask her, as she cooks my favorite Thai dish, if she is imitating ZZ Moon.

She sets the table perfectly, lights a pink candle, serves us, and pours the water with ice and lemon slices. She's been nicer since going out with the guy from the gym.

"Are you doing any better, babe?" she asks.

"A little. Yeah, I guess." I eat the perfect golden-crusted morsels of tofu, dipping them in the green chili sauce that no one else can make. Curry, lemongrass, cilantro, coconut milk, toasted cumin, tons of green chili paste. "Ma, this is good."

She leans across the table and pats my hand. "Thanks," she says. It's easy to be with her tonight. Maybe this is just Ma healthy. Ma at the rare right balance of hormones, pharmaceuticals, neurotransmitters. Poor old Ma. I'm on the edge of the old feeling I had when I was little and she was my world. I'm on the edge of jumping off and loving her again. I almost want to tell her about Orpheus. I want to tell her something. I want to give her something.

I look at the work on my left hand—the usual dense arrangement of daily messages to myself, sketched faces, symbols.

She looks at my hand at the same time. "It's so beautiful," she says, getting lost in the flow of symbols.

As we rode down the elevator that morning, there was a moment when we looked at each other. I could have been shy, seeing him in this context, both of us clothed and out of the bed where we'd just been so intimate—but my tiredness dissolved the strangeness. I was weak, leaning on him.

He reached up and took a tug at the thick, quiltlike swathe of insulating padding lining the elevator. It was partially hanging, ugly, and came loose easily. He pulled some more, and some more, and then the whole huge swathe of padding came undone, like an ugly quilt. He wrapped it around us while I protested and screamed.

I caught my breath. "Just one thing," I said.

"Any one thing," he said, squeezing the spot where my shoulder curves into my neck, melting the awkwardness.

"If you wanted to see me again, why didn't you do something when I showed up with my sister, that time on the roof? You didn't even try to be with me."

"I didn't say I was obsessed with seeing you again," he said. "I was obsessed with the idea that I wouldn't see you again. When you showed up, I didn't know what to do."

"But the next time?" We were at the ground floor.

"The next time, you knew what to do." He laughed his low laugh. And he kissed me there with the stiff material around us like a bizarre landscape and the elevator doors stupidly opening and closing.

I'll find you, he said. Only he doesn't.

He's been back from his tour for two weeks and I've read his diary every day and there is no mention of me. He's posted some pictures and I recognize one from the party— the two girls posed raunchily by him on the couch. No sign of what we had. It takes me a little while to realize that he's disappeared, because I've been in pain over Zack and because it simply seems impossible. What I experienced with him—what we shared that night and that morning— couldn't just be thrown away. Somehow there's a mistake.

That first kiss, in his bed. We were kissing tenderly, with a gentleness, a sweetness, and then—there was a delicious shift, as if a new substance had rolled in between us, changing the density of the molecules in the air, slowing our organs. We looked into each other, breathing. It had everything to do with breath, with the scent—it was such a severe magic. Did Moon know about this, I wondered, and then she passed out of my thoughts and he became all.

One winter day, way before I met Orpheus, I went with Ma to get the car fixed and I was bored, so I walked around the frozen reservoir near the garage. There was a wide promenade running for a few miles alongside the reservoir; in sunny weather it would be filled with bikers and skaters.

On that day there was just me and one family off in the distance. It was cold, the sky a flat silver, the reservoir covered with snow. There was nothing to look at. I pulled the hood of my coat tight over my head even though it made an annoying sound with every step I took. I walked this way with the coat and my own thoughts jostling in my ears for about a mile and then I decided to stretch.

I went over to the rail and gazed out at the pure, white, unbroken sweep of snow. Pieces of ice with the faintest tint of blue had frozen in a wave pattern. Beyond that, for miles, was just the silky plane of snow, ending in a straight line at the horizon, sharp and black as if it had been drawn with Japanese ink.

Everything was sharper in the crystalline air, and the sight before me was enormous. It wasn't just the visual aspect of beauty, but the way the snow and mountains and color of the sky played together, the way they were so alive and so quiet.

What amazed me was it had been here all along. I had thought there was nothing to look at. It was as if I had passed through a membrane of dumbness and now dwelled on the other side.

The family was close now and loud.

A little boy was repeatedly saying something he had obviously learned from a TV or movie character. "So, you think you are so clever!" he kept saying. I wanted him to shut up. I wanted them all to notice the miraculous sight. And in wanting it I slipped back to the other side of the membrane. I could still see it was beautiful, as I walked back, but I saw it like you would see the flat image of a picture postcard; its beauty no longer held all my attention. Only because all my attention did not hold its beauty.

The alchemy of that kiss made me pass through the membrane of dumbness, but of course that is obvious and redundant and something which could be said only by someone who had passed back again.

The pain is unexpected and searing, like stepping barefoot on a wasp. It takes me a while to realize that of course something has happened to keep him from contacting me. It could be as simple as losing my e-mail or maybe he's frightened by the intensity. It's possible he wants to post something on his website to me but can't because of the publicity. Agnes has heard enough of these theories.

"Come on, Anooshka, he's a dirtbag player." Agnes is leaning close so we don't disturb the concentration of the simple-faced blond girl onstage in the Woodstock Cafe. The people in front are bobbing their heads, exercising their bland brains. We're sitting at a back table and I don't care about breaking the pleasant spell; neither does Raphael.

"He's a coke addict," he says, loudly, drawing dirty glances from the couple next to us. "Don't you get it?"

I feel a swelling hatred for Raphael, for Agnes, for the girl onstage, her bland innocence, strumming her guitar, singing in her inconsequential voice. The hate slashes through me to the point where I can imagine heaving our table over, sending splintered glasses into the crowd, breaking their rapt silence. I feel tight as a trigger just before it's pulled all the way back.

"I gotta go," I tell my pals, standing, all of us knowing there's nowhere to go. They follow me out, though, into the cooled-down evening, the stars hard and bright, the crickets loud. It doesn't help that Raphael and Agnes are hooked up now and can't walk without their arms all over each other and keep looking at each other in that weird new way. We start walking, following the cracked sidewalk toward the cemetery.

"You're really fucked up over this," Raphael says.

"No kidding, man," says Agnes.

"It was real, though," I tell them. "We spent every second talking. He was worried when I looked sad. I mean, he cared."

Their faces are frozen in cynical masks.

"He said I could trust him!"

"Oh," says Agnes. "Why didn't you say so? That gives us a whole new perspective."

Raph gives her a sharp look. "Come on, he obviously felt something for her. . . ."

"Yeah," I say, warming to his empathy. "I feel like he's lost." I don't know how to tell them about our connection; like certain phenomena, it resists analysis and proofs. There are different times during the day when I absolutely know he's thinking about me. I feel like he's summoning me, silently telling me how much he longs for me, too. I keep thinking of what he said at the hotel party: "We'll know when the time is right." We were both able to sense each other's deepest, subtlest needs—but if I try to tell this to these guys, they will think it's reality TV.

We sit with our backs propped on ancient tombstones. I shake off the annoyance of Raph's hand interlaced in Agnes's. I hate units.

"It's an intangible communication," I start. "I feel like he needs—"

"He needs someone to kick his ass," says Raphael. "And I'll do it."

Agnes laughs. "Yeah, you hold him down and I'll pimp slap him."

Then she sees my face. "Come on—we're kidding."

"I'm not," says Raphael. "Look what he did to our girl."

Self-pity gathers in my throat.

"Oh, come on, she's not in love with that scummy nerdboy," says Agnes.

"You're sick from it, Nu." Raphael goes as if to touch my face and I pull back. I hate them discussing me like a patient. "You have blue dents under your eyes."

"And look at this—" Agnes picks up my wrist, displays my arm for Raphael. "Look at her poor arm; it's like a stick. She doesn't eat food; she's living off her guts."

"That's not love," says Raphael.

I slide down onto the grave, curling up with my ear pressed to the dirt, listening for some word. "I'm depressed because I miss Zack." It's true and it takes the edge off the Orpheus thing.

"Crazy girl," Raphael says fondly.

"Barking mad," says Agnes, stroking my head.

The next morning I get a present from Moon in the mail. Like something you'd find on a divine creature—a many-stranded necklace with hundreds of seed-sized beads in variant tones of blue, incorporated with Zack's luminescent feathers. "This might be ghoulish," she wrote on a Post-it note. "But I think it suits you."

I'm on the old, musty couch on the porch, my face pressed into the pillows. Ma's gone. Or I thought she was until she's suddenly sitting right by me, hand on my wet cheek. I bolt up.

"Shit, Ma, what are you doing?"

She doesn't react, just gazes at me with a purity in her gaze—a look I haven't seen in years, so clear and compassionate, no trace of pity. It goes into my chest, that look, and I almost lean into her.

"Sweetheart," she says. "I know all about it. Moon told me."

A zigzag of craziness goes through me. I stand up like some kind of stung beast. But there's nowhere to turn, nowhere to go. And I haven't told Moon the whole story, so what could she tell. Bluffing, Ma's bluffing.

Ma tugs at my hand. "You can sit. Sit with me, Nu, I want to be there for you."

I'm so numb I just do it. And then the weirdest freak thing happens.

"You really fell for him, didn't you?"

I actually tell her yes.

"You fell deeply."

"Yeah," I say, and it's a relief to tell her.

"You saw the best in him and he seemed like an angel to you; everything else melted away. . . ."

"I guess. . . ."

"Don't you get it," says Ma, tender as a lamb. "That's not love, baby. It's obsession. You're just projecting. You're reenacting stuff that happened with your dad. When you're obsessed and infatuated all you see is the good."

"Exactly. And that's love." I want to shake her small skull. I stand up and lean against the porch rail, gripping it with my hands so hard it feels like the wood's going to snap.

"But Anooshka, when that fades away two days later, when reality sets in, how can you call that love? Love is devotion."

"Really?" I tell her. "How do you know? Who was ever devoted to you? Who were you ever devoted to? You've been with what—eighteen or nineteen junkies, married guys, alcoholics, abusive nuts—"

"That's enough, Anooshka—"

"No, you're gonna listen. And you want to tell me,

what—that love is really about, what? Cooking for someone every day? Nightly blow jobs? Holding their hand when they die? Changing their diapers when they get Alzheimer's? Just sticking it out? Yeah, because you've done that, right?"

Ma hasn't moved. Her nose is turning pink and her eyes are filling up. I thought she'd get pissed. Didn't expect this.

"I'm saying I want more for you," she says softly. And then it just hits me. All those moments when Ma's eyes were all lit up, singing the praises of some creep, she really loved him. I saw her for a moment in a holy perspective, I saw all of us as misguided martyrs, the way we held all these wackos in the highest light, blind to all their bad stuff.

I sit down and sling my arm around her tiny shoulders. "Oh Ma, and I'm just saying that you get what you get. And maybe everything you had with all those lunatics, maybe that was how you loved. I mean, it was. That was love. You've loved all your life."

"But it's codependence, it's sickness. You can't call that love."

"Ma, I loved him. We had a real connection."

"Then where is he?"

"It doesn't matter."

But of course it does.

Snake driver

"This heat," I say to the driver. *Even though the weather is meaningless now that I'm blocks away from Orpheus.*

"I am just coming back from New Delhi and this is nothing," says the driver.

"Are you Hindu?" I say.

"Yes," he says, "I am."

"Can I ask you something?"

"You can ask anything."

"I mean if it's too rude or—"

"Anything is okay," he insists.

"See, my bird just died and I was wondering, do you believe a bird can become a human?"

"Oh yes," says the driver. "Any animal can become any animal or even a human. It is very possible."

I wanted to know that there could be something more for him, but of course, who says a human is a step up?

I showed up at Moon's that morning and we lay on her bed and I told her everything about the time with Orpheus. She stroked my forehead. Looking into her wide, soft eyes, I felt utter acceptance.

"And Moon, he said that it takes time to get to know someone. He said it like we were going to get to know each other."

"Oh Nooshk, how could anyone not love you?"

At moments like that I'm so at peace with my sister, I have the comforting sensation of a double heart and double mind.

"In fact," says the driver, "I was a cobra in my last life."

"You're kidding."

"No, I am not. My mother told me all about it. She was trying to stop the neighbor from killing a snake. And the neighbor killed the snake anyway, but before it died it looked my mother right in the eyes and she felt that look deep inside of herself."

"Wow."

"And my mother, she had seven girls before she had me and was always praying for a boy. That night, the night the snake was killed, my mother became pregnant."

I left Moon's and took pictures of trees in an East Village park, until a deep twilight fell. An ecstatic bird sang out, with clean silver notes, expressed so freely. All the birds started up then, the cooing, the warbles, the flutey trills, all the good-byes sung to the sun from the tops of trees. Shadows scattered in dark shapes on the ground and the trees grew black, but between them there was golden light.

Then the darkness covered everything, birds, leaves, trees.

The park's somewhere near his building, a building I would never recognize because I wasn't paying attention. How could that have been possible? Earlier in the day I walked in his neighborhood, seeking familiar balconies, his beautiful face—I could see his eyes so close to mine, the shifting light within them, the feeling of him, the alteration of the air we breathed as we moved into each other. I searched the street, holding my loaded camera, ready. But it didn't happen.

After the park I went back to Moon's and we drank ginseng sodas. Then she left me alone in her apartment to go off with Marley; this time she absolutely had to know where I would go, even though I promised her I was tired and wouldn't get into trouble. Still, she gave me her usual speech: "And don't dream of going out, blah blah. I'll be calling you later, blah." I waited five minutes and then ran down to get the cab.

"She became pregnant and what do you think? *Now look at my skin. Look."*

He holds his right hand up and I see its coarse, scaly quality. *"I am sixty-eight years old!"* he says, with a crazy giggle. *"Yes, it is true!"*

"You look young," I tell him. His face is not old. Or snaky. Big grin. Brown eyes. A relaxed aura.

We are at my street. *"You look twenty years younger,"* I say.

"That is because I have good, strong snake skin," he says. *"Never anything wrong with my skin in all these years. I was definitely the cobra! Go ahead, touch it."*

"That's okay," I say, handing him the money. *"But thank you for all the information."*

"Thank you for listening," he says. *"Most people do not."*

The first shock is when the door to Constellation doesn't open immediately. Then I hear the buzz and push. At the desk I pull out my ID and go to sign in the book and the woman, blank faced, efficient, composed, says: "No underage people without accompaniment."

"But I've been here before," I tell her. "I know Orpheus."

Just the corners of her mouth lift; she's transparently relishing this moment of her power. "If he's sent for you, your name will be on the list—"

She knows he hasn't. But maybe he has. I don't want to give her my name. But what if he's been waiting for me?

"Can't you just call him—" And then—"Wait, is he here now? Because I can call him, if you let me use—"

"Honey—you are not going to use my phone."

She presses the buzzer and in walks the London man with the neat rows. He doesn't know me at first and then he's all like: "Girl, how's it all doin'?" and he tells the woman: "She's cool, we know her." To me: "He'll be chuffed to see you, come on up."

In the elevator I feel nervous but I know it's going to be good. I'll find out all the answers when he sees me again—when we see each other. The weirdness will disappear; I'll forgive him. I'll tell him about Zack—I can still hear him saying: What, my darling, your bird?

"You look happy, puppy," says the man. "I remember you now—you were the shy one. He liked you. I'm doing a good thing here. He'll be glad I took care of you now."

"Thanks." It feels real now, at last, in the elevator. Only a few more seconds of wondering what I'll say to him, what he'll say to me. I'm wearing the clothes I wore when I hooked up with him that night—even Moon's sandals. To provoke his memory? Mine? The only thing different is the necklace with Zack's feathers and the clothes are looser on me, as if I've put them on after a long bout with illness.

I see him right away, at the bar, back to us, talking to someone. Just wait here a sec, London Man tells me, parking me by a potted tree. Orpheus tosses a glance back at me and throws a frustrated gesture at London Man. Everything is so wrong. I can only think he doesn't know me. Or if I wait, if I'm patient, maybe he'll get out of this intense conversation, maybe a record deal, it could be anything, he wasn't expecting me—

"I'm sorry, sugarsnap." London Man puts a hand on my shoulder as if to steer me out of there. "It's such a bad time, I didn't realize—he said he'd love to see you—well, when things aren't so crazy, you know?"

Orpheus is getting up, moving toward us, throws me an empty nodding smile, and heads toward the kitchen. I break off from my escort and go after Orpheus. "Wait—"

Impatience flares in his eyes. Then strained tolerance. He does not want to be standing there. Everything's pulling him away except for this one momentary annoyance that must be dealt with, and that's me.

"But what happened?" He looks at me like I'm a window and there's nothing much to see on the other side.

"I'll be right back," he says, and disappears into the kitchen. And does not come back.

24. Honey Just Kill Me

*It doesn't matter / things will change / it's static chatter /
you're home on the range / life seems dire / but you're still
alive*

—from "It Doesn't Matter," © ORPHEUS XTIIMUSIC

I can't tell anyone.

I'm in bed, fully awake, listening to the phone ring,
knowing it's Moon, not picking up the first time in my
life.

"Nu, you up?" I barely feel the traitor, lying there
listening to her message. "Okay, sweetie, good night."

I don't want Moon to know I broke the rules again,
but more, I don't want her to know I was humiliated—no,
it's not even that. I don't want her to convince me, in any
way, that his actions have proved he isn't to be loved.

Some nights I can't get to sleep for hours and others I wake
at three or four with a raw alarm inside, like now. I go to
the computer and find his latest diary.

Orpheus Online
programmed beings

a demented mother mouse teaches baby mouse to find a
mate you have to break your little foot and hop around in the
middle of a field even though the hawks could find you there
and kill you.

the mouse comes to believe that to find love it has to do ridicu-
lous things that put its life in danger. our little mouse from a
demented mother hops about the field, his little foot hurting,
but still he is feeling hopeful. hop, hop, maybe I will find a
mate. i will try hard this time and it will definitely happen.

in the moment that the hawk swoops down, the mouse, mis-
taking him for the mate, feels a swooning, a freedom, a joy,
utter bliss.

it is so ironic that we can feel the *most* free and joyful when we
are acting from the most ingrained, programmed behaviors. our
parents press this button and that button, industrious little computer programmers. they praise us extravagantly and then they
call us nasty names. 10 years later we meet someone who
praises us extravagantly and calls us nasty names . . . voilà they
have pressed the exact right buttons and unlocked the door to
our hard drive. and now we are soaring, feeling free.

this time is different, we say to ourselves, every time, until the time the hawk swoops down and we close our eyes in bliss and we whisper, honey just kill me now.

Who did that to him? I read it again, again, until I have it playing inside me.

This morning I'm crying before I open my eyes. Something's happened to me. A heaviness. The world is toned down five notches, as if I pressed a mute button. I'm exhausted. My limbs feel injected with toxins.

"You're depressed," Ma informs me that afternoon, with a tinge of distaste, like my hair needs fixing. It's not me, though. The world really is the way I'm seeing it. I was deluded before, when I was too happy; then I saw things with a false sheen. Things are, in reality, random and senseless, boring and brutal.

At certain times I think I hear Zack singing in the woods. First from one tree, then another, as if all the other birds are using his voice.

I think about writing to Orpheus through a chat room on his site. Dear Orpheus, remember? Each day I could remind him of something we did that night, something he said. Or I could just write something cryptic and poetic to get his attention:

I think of you when—

I want to calm your heart—

I want to tame the wild look in your—

Nothing would work. Everything's trite. I could understand why he didn't want to speak to me after we'd been so close. Because life would only be disappointing from there.

I fall asleep holding the black plastic lighter he gave me on the bus that night. It was so close to his hand.

I'm a thin balloon filled with water, punctured in pieces. I'm on the old musty-smelling couch on the porch one afternoon, crying because there is no escape—

And then Ma's there, kneeling beside me. "What is it?" she asks.

I stiffen, straighten up, can't stand her pushy, intrusive face.

"Nothing, I'm fine."

"Please tell me, baby," she says. "Nooshka, don't you understand you're my baby?"

"Don't you understand—it's none of your business."

She starts to cry. "But you used to tell me everything." That has never been true under any circumstance.

"It's nothing," I say again.

"Anooshka—" She fixes me with what she probably

imagines is a maternal, searching look. "Are you pregnant?"

"No," I tell her. I got my period only a few days ago. And with it, a faint wave of regret.

I see a phantom Zack sometimes, especially at night, a quick light moving through the room, out of the corner of my eye. Stop going so fast, I tell it. Take a solid form. At least come to me in my dreams. None of that happens.

So, I'm at another party with Raphael. People are doing slimy lime Jell-O tequila shots and tonight I have nothing to lose.

Another party

"Don't," says Raphael.

"Whatever," I tell him. "It's summer. Let me have fun." He sticks around in spite of my attitude. He's even hovering, hours later, when I'm in the pool in my underwear and Scarlett swims up under me and slides her hands up between my legs and pinches my ass. If I wasn't drunk I might drown her, but tonight I just laugh. "Lesbian." I say it affectionately, but it only sharpens the strangely excited look on her face. I notice her breasts—hard not to, inches from my face—nearly round and slightly falling with their weight.

"Actually, I thought you were one, until I heard Orpheus did you."

"What—"

"That's okay, he did me, too."

The tequila in my blood blunts the knife of her words, and it doesn't seem so bad that we were both with Orpheus. I grin at her with boozy camaraderie; we're sisters through the flesh.

"Come on," says Raphael, trying to hoist me out of the water.

"No way," I tell him. "This is getting good."

"Does this sound familiar," says Scarlett, shifting her voice to a low, hypnotic cadence. *"You're so perfect. Are you my angel? You must be a messenger."*

I feel an alarm inside, panic rising. *"This is not a nor-*

mal thing that has happened between us, you know that," she persists, saying it just like he said it to me. I didn't repeat those words to anyone.

"Shut up. Shut up! He told you he said that to me?" The betrayal is sobering as a slap.

"No, he didn't tell me," says Scarlett. Then she shifts into the voice again, taunting me: *"I recognized you the moment I first saw you. I could spot you in a room of thousands because you would see me seeing you."*

"Who did he tell—" For a second I can't remember her name, the girl in all the photos, the one leaning on him at Constellation, the one who's friends with Scarlett. He must have told her—Durgha, that was it—he must have told Durgha all about our night, and Durgha must have told Scarlett. Wait, maybe that means it was special to him, to talk about it.

"You're not getting what I'm saying to you." She gets up so close to me in the water, I can smell the sweetish burned pot odor of her breath and feel the rubbery tips of her breasts against me. I back off. "He said the same things to me, that's how I know."

That night—that morning, actually—at three, I'm in the jeep with Raphael, insane. *Help me,* I've been saying to him for hours.

"I am helping you," he says in a monotone. He's taken

me to the ATM, waited for me to grab some things from my house, has spent hours trying to talk me out of this, and is now driving me all the way to Poughkeepsie to catch a five A.M. train to the city. I need Moon. Raphael almost cries when I get on the train. I'm just going to see my sister, I assure him. You know she's the only one who can help me.

I'm hugging myself on the train, rocking to dispel my jittery energy, alone in the car, too early even for the commuters. I've cried until there's nothing. I don't call Moon; I don't have to, she'll just be there.

Only she's not. I let myself in with my key and suck in the air of her empty place in the early light, everything so still and nice and clean. The wooden floor is cool on my feet. I walk around and really look at the things on her walls that I'm so used to—the biscuit-colored sculptures of bone and seaweed and beach clay; the light falling through the open window onto the bed, with its deep purple spread and tassled pillows. The green gauzy swathe of fabric attached above to create a sense of canopy. When I lie on the bed I see only the sky out the window, looking extra bright with my oncoming hangover, the clouds fast moving and close as if they might come into the window. I walk around touching things. I sit at her desk. And then I see a neat stack of pages printed out from her computer. The first one is an Orpheus diary, an old one, about the Orpheus myth. My heart starts a slow march.

Orpheus Online
New York
dude blew it

at some point he can't stand it anymore. he has ached for her so long. he has to know if it is really her. he needs more than the contact of her hand in his. what if it is someone else's hand? the desire to see her dear face is unbearable. so he looks. and euridyce dies for the second and last time and orpheus fucking blew it.

orpheus

I flip to the next one.

Orpheus Online
New York
lutedreams

every myth has tiny little secrets stuffed inside. if there is a snakebite in a myth it might mean sex. or the snake could just be knowledge, a big old coil of DNA, the blueprint of our existence, whatever it is that takes us down from the heights and lands us in this human form.

it's amazing that people in white togas and lace-up sandals and golden chariots were having the same dreams as those of us zooming about in our cars with our ears attached to phones, all of us little orpheuses and euridyces, trying to make deals with the underworld, making impossible bargains to keep love alive.

With a sense of doom, I tear through the stack. The diaries are in chronological order; I read some only days ago. All of them are about obsession. I search through them, craving reasons for his emotional disappearance. That Moon has them—here is another mystery, one that feels so wrong. I want to leave her apartment, but it's a small impulse, drowned by this strange hour, no sleep, still being partly drunk, feeling like an exhausted animal and too gritty to move.

In her bathroom I shake on the toilet, catch myself looking frightened and deranged in the mirror—hair twisted with the chlorine from the pool, mascara pooled beneath one eye. I go back to her desk. My heart's jittery and I fight the impulse to lie down on a square of sunlight on her floor.

In this state there is a delicate peeling back and the air of the room, the sky through the window, my own hands, the papers on the desk, become linked, taking on a hyper-reality. Her chair holds me as his words tug me down into the darkest place. It seems impossible that he could write them before we met:

Orpheus Online
infatuation

it seems to be about the specific point of connection. it seems to be about a certain person. it seems *so much* to be about a certain person. their eyes, the color nowhere in nature. their smell, like a gray melody. the way only they leaned into you. the way they felt when you were pressed up against each other. But how can it be about someone specific when the feeling is always the same.

The euphoria, the longing, the melting, the sense of home, the loss of appetite, as if everything shuts down but the love receptors. As if all your nourishment can now come from the beloved, a feeling ancient as the infant brain:

Ah Mother, feed me!

This feeling is so universal it's in every love song. That's why we can all identify, can all cry to the pop songs whether we're rich old men or cute teenage girls. It is the *same* feeling for all of us and built into this feeling is the sense of the specific. I feel *this way* because of *him only*. I feel this *amazing way* because *she* is the only one who can make me feel *this way*.

Orpheus Online
the curse of forgetting

the heart opens and then it breaks and then it heals up like a gash in the skin, so completely you might remember there had once been a sensitivity, a feeling, but now there is *nothing*, smooth territory, ready to be broken again as if for the first time. the flip side of that is that it is possible to be made whole again even after you are broken wide open.

The curse is also the ability.

And then I read the last one:

Orpheus Online
programmed beings

a demented mother mouse teaches baby mouse to find a mate . . .

I don't need to read the words, because I know them, but I let my eyes absorb them anyway, again, masochistic little rodent.

... this time is different, we say to ourselves, every time, until
the time the hawk swoops down and we close our eyes in bliss
and we whisper, honey just kill me now.

And I think, yes, that's how it is. He's just like me.

When Moon comes home, I'm asleep with my head on
the desk.

"I was doing it for you," she says, but we've never been
able to lie to each other. There's a defensiveness in the way
she's standing, in the strained tone of her voice, which
infects me with the bitter victory of a wife finally meeting
the mistress. "I was gathering—I was trying to collect some
kind of proof about how calculating he is. About his whole
demented personality."

"Moon, you're full of shit—"

"I didn't trust him—"

"Why?"

"That night—" She stops herself. "I didn't want to tell
you." She kneels beside me, her eyes gentle. I want to kick
her. Haven't felt this way since we were so small, fighting
on the floor, pulling each other's hair, trying to kill each
other, over the contested ownership of a bottle of orange
glitter nail polish.

I get off the chair, go to the window. The sky's
warm and flat white.

"Why didn't you trust him?" My voice is calm, but my hands go into fists. I remember the night of the party now, that moment when she got strange.

"Did you do something with him?"

I expect a quick denial, but her hesitation makes me sick. I grab my stuff off the floor, start heading for the door. "It's not like that, Nooshka," she says, blocking me. "Stop for a second and I'll tell you what happened."

I've got the door opened, waiting. I hate the scent of flowers rising from her. I hate her emerald cat eyeliner, her pink mouth. I hate her perfect being, always the one, never me, even now, taking him.

"He just came on to me, that's all."

"You're lying—I was there the whole time—"

"No, Nu," she says, even softer. "We went into the bathroom; I thought we were going to do some lines—"

"You don't do coke."

"That night—things were bad with Marley, everything was so—"

"So screwed up because I was the one he liked?"

"No, I was happy for you—"

"Yeah, so happy you—" and suddenly I remember being at the party during that one aimless moment, feeling lost, not being able to find either of them. He was in the bathroom with her, kissing her.

I'm out the door, running—

"Nothing happened," she says. "I swear on everything . . . it was just that it could've. I would never . . ." She grabs me and she's stronger still, grabs me and spins me around. "Listen to me."

We're on the landing, facing off, both of us on such an edge we could push each other down the stairs.

"You're my sister, my best friend—you can't be with someone who sings like that, writes like that—"

"Why, because you can't?"

This one landed, and I can see the hurt in her eyes. She goes on anyway, like she really loves me. "Because all the brilliant ones—they can sing it and they can paint it, but they can't do it. You can't expect them to love you."

"So you have to be with the ones who can't talk at all, who have nothing, like Marley, right?"

"He's not like that." She lets go of me. "You know, you're a bitch, Anooshka. I was looking that stuff up to try to help you."

"I don't want your help." She says nothing, and I say it again, louder, like a maniac, feeling the sound tear up my throat: "I don't want your fucking help!" I go down the stairs, not waiting for her to stop me.

I go to the river park near Moon's place, standing at one of the city's edges, looking at New Jersey. Take in the early morning city noise: joggers talking to each other in pant breaths, wail of a baby in a stroller, barking dog, street noise of squealing truck brakes, distant ambulance whine. Underneath it there's an unidentifiable drone, the sound of this sad existence.

I have nowhere to go, so I'm going home. At the bus station the piped-in music is upbeat, a light reggae that spits on my darkness. And then it shifts, so subtly it takes me a few beats to register, into Orpheus. I have that sinister, unreal sensation of things closing in, my heart beating faster, the sense of being looked at, afraid I'll black out, here in the station, spiraling down, head hitting concrete, people parting around my body. I have to leave, I have to leave, I go out into the streets and it's worse out there, the air thick and stagnant as if it's been breathed in and out by a trillion pairs of lungs. I want out of the disconnected business of the humans, ears attached to their cell phones, moving on their preordained tracks like ants.

I'm the only being running without direction or purpose, looking for a sign, I'll follow the first sign, God help me, show me a sign, show me a way, give me a place—

And there it is, an arrow. And I follow it down.

25. The Invisible Ones

Underground

*Some bruises go so deep / they never rise to the surface /
can't you make that leap / to the solitary circus*

—from "High Wire," © ORPHEUS XTIIMUSIC

I probably wouldn't have stayed down there if Odessa
hadn't found me immediately. She was on a wooden bench
like anyone waiting for a train, only she had a broken,
rope-tied suitcase, bulging with the usual bag lady accou-
trements: rags, newspapers, useless scraps and materials.

Her face looked normal. I noticed her makeup and her clear gaze and her combed hair.

"You don't have to be scared," she told me, and that was what did it, because I was terrified and no one else was looking at me or into my eyes or telling me not to be scared. She lugged her bag over to the wall, stashing it behind a trash can. "I'll just leave this here for a sec."

We got on a train and took it to the place where it curves deeply in the tunnel just before it heads into Grand Central. You get off there and then there's a spot *they* know about.

It's such a bright new world for a place underground. It's more like a clean youth hostel than a homeless shelter, although there is nowhere for Odessa and me to sleep. Some people have built shelters they call their houses, and in this one tunnel they're lined up like houses on a street. You can stand up inside them. At night they have a meal for themselves and put out a meal for the rats laced with rat poison.

The only thing to do in this subterranean world is talk, watch out for the rats and crackheads, and find things to eat. No one pisses there, no one smokes. This is the place people go to when they're in between, when they have to hide. No one knows about this place above. They've heard, but no one comes into this tunnel without a reference.

Then how did you take me in? I ask Odessa. Because, baby, you were referred by God.

Sound of a woman's orgasm. Fake, according to my father. I'm eight, sitting on my suitcase by the front door. He's in the next room with a bottle of whiskey and blown-up pictures of his lover tacked to the walls.

"You hear this part, Anooshka?" The moaning gets louder.

"Yeah, I hear it. Dad, Ma's going to be here soon. . . ."

I close my eyes and whistle for Zack, put him in his cage.

My father comes out carrying the tape recorder. The moaning picks up speed, gets out of hand. We've heard it a few times. "You see? The bitch was lying to me even then!"

He hits the rewind button and the moaning starts up again just as Ma arrives to take Moon and me away, tooting the horn. I open the door and the California sunshine blots out everything. . . .

"And that's the last time I saw him—well, one more time, a few years later when we met at an airport."

"So he made this tape."

"Right."

"And he was always taping the women he had relationships with?"

"Them, me, whatever. He liked to tape. He's creative. Now he makes videos."

"And you don't think that might have something to do with why you don't believe in love?"

"The videos?"

"You can joke, but you might want to consider the role your father played."

"Nah," I say. "If it had to be a parent, it would be my mother. But it's really about this bird. And this guy."

Odessa has lived below forever, she says. We're riding on an F train, talking between five-minute sleeps. She says I'm happy because I'm in a manic state. She thinks I have a chemical imbalance. I say I don't care as long as I'm not depressed. Oh, don't worry, she says, you will be again. Takes one to know one.

If you've been here forever, then why do you look so good? I say. She's been wearing a fresh new outfit every day, unlike me. My clothes are beginning to grow stiff with dirt.

Why do I look so good? says Odessa. That's a good question. And I'm gonna tell you the answer: because I'm a liar. Of course I haven't been down here forever. I go up every day.

She's a mystery, and I don't care. She's just always with me and we travel train to train and she talks to me. Maybe because I haven't slept, or maybe because I've crossed over the edge of sanity, I tell her things, and things I thought were buried keep coming up like delicate frog bubbles.

"Do you think I should have gone with him?"

"When did he give you the chance?"

"The morning we said good-bye, outside my sister's. I thought he was joking when he said why don't you come with me. But what if I'd said yes?"

"Let's think about that on the next train."

"And when you went out to your ma's car, that was it, you just walked into the bright California sunshine and there was nothing else but the ride home with your mama?"

And then I see it, what happened in between. It doesn't come as a surprise, not as a recovered shocking memory like people who were molested. It comes back as something I've always known but not thought about too much.

"Last chance, Nu," my father says to me. "You can come with me to India. I'll teach you to play

the sitar, or whatever. They have little blue gods with six arms there. We'll make a treehouse in the magic jungle. . . ."

He turns down the sound of his cheating lover's orgasm to make the pitch.

I have my stuff packed in my denim suitcase, and the reality of the suitcase means I am already going. Plus—Ma. I need her. I want to go with my father, but Ma—she's my ma; she might die in her bed if I don't come back. And Moon, she's going to live with Ma; I need Moon. I shake my head no. I don't feel anything; I have nothing to say. He lifts me and groans at my weight. My face is mashed against his shoulder, smelling his scent of aftershave and Camel cigarettes, as a pain twists through me like a river. He sets me down.

And then Ma's honking outside.

My father hoists my suitcase, takes my hand in his big warm hand, walks me out. Before he puts me in the car, he says: "Be tough now, kid. You made a good choice and stick with it. Don't look back and you'll be okay."

"So you realize," says Odessa, "that the choice was not really yours."

"Please don't tell me any more," I say. The empty place

in my chest, the blank spot, is just a hard scar. I start to remember the songs Dad sent me from India, the sound samples. I threw them out. The scar starts to melt a little and hurt like hell. I wasn't the one who made him go away.

It's okay to look back if you can stand it. Maybe he's looked back a few times, too.

Moon's place

I emerge one night, filthy, people really looking at me now. But the world's kinder. I was only down there four or five days, but everything has changed. I call ZZ and wake her. I go to her place and there are no words between us.

We go to hug and she backs off at my filth, then embraces me anyway. I stand in the shower, blast the heat, sit in the stall, let it pound my brains out.

"I'm better now," I tell her. And there's nothing more to be said about that.

Of course Odessa was not tangible. I'm not psychotic. No human could be that good. But sometimes it's the invisible ones who take you to a place that heals.

The French diner's plain and austere in that shockingly rich European way. Even at two A.M. you can get a twenty-eight-dollar trout. It's quiet as hell, and it's cool and white, with dull chrome, like a retro medicine cabinet. The people sitting in the old red leather booths at the low chrome tables all have things in their hands or beside their plates: phones, magazines, pens, mirrors. It's amazing how quickly I can adjust to being aboveground.

There is no music. Our coffees are black and sweet, and we are on our third ones. The mood is so subdued it's as if we have all lost our pets. Our loves have left us without explanation.

"He's still a scumbag," says Moon. It's a relief to love her face again: her most serious gray eyes, her wide mouth, her eyebrows covering only half her eyes, the rest shaved. "Oh little sweetie, you're so tired."

Such a honey husky voice. Such good licorice basil perfume. "What are you wearing?" someone asked her once, in the back of a movie theater. "Oh, just some French shit," she said. I was so proud of her for saying that so effortlessly. I never heard her say it again. I always wanted to say those same words if someone would just ask me what I was wearing. I tried once or twice during the time when I wore a light grapefruit scent and people scrunched their noses, wanting to know. It sounded so crude and practiced when I said it.

"I love your perfume," I tell her now, resting my forehead against her cool, bare forearm.

"You nut," she says, stroking my head. "It's probably my pits you're smelling anyway."

I lay my head on my folded arms and shut my eyes and feel, for this first moment, that I am now going to sleep forever.

How I miss Zack, even in this diner. Even underground, where he would never be. When they die, you begin to miss them at times and in contexts that you never would before, as if their non-presence now extends to everywhere. There in the diner, clean and aboveground, I imagine life turning fresh, in a hazy way, as if you are at last in the garden with your real mother, the one you didn't have this time, the one who was always there anyway, the one who reached you in tiny ways every day, through the veil of pain, in the form of a tiny little blue bird, for example, through his tiny kind eyes looking at you with such compassion every day of your life. And singing his songs, his mothering songs.

26. Hollywood Ending

The Zen is a hateful place in the winter. The snow keeps the tourists away, and the ski people eat at the resorts. You can hang around all night and get three tables if you're lucky. And if you're not lucky, you can get one table with Scarlett sitting at the head.

My hand shakes as I pour her water.

"Have you washed your hands?" she asks me, loud enough for the others at the table.

I don't answer.

"I just have this thing about germs," she says to her androgynous girlfriend. The girl nods.

"Scarlett, you are over the top," Lindsay scolds, throwing me an apologetic smile.

"We haven't seen you lately," Scarlett says.

Nope, they haven't. We stopped going to Lindsay's parties at the end of the summer. Missed the Halloween bash where Sean got picked up for a DWI on the way home. Heard they had oysters flown in from Cape Cod for their New Year's festivities. Next week is the Valentine's party, and Lindsay's parents will be off in St. Martin. We will not be going to that, either.

Agnes has been busy with Raph, and I have rented a thousand DVDs.

They say you become what you do, and if all you do is watch movies, you begin to see your life like one. I've got a Hollywood ending I can't get out of my head, and it's helped me through the season.

The Romantic Redemptive Hollywood Ending

ANOOSHKA'S ISLAND—DAY

A deep blue sky, one cloud drifting. We move lazily across the sky and then down and down, taking in the lush, wild surroundings of ANOOSHKA's secret island in the middle of the river: a tiny outcropping of purple and yellow flowers shielded by tough saplings. The river's rushing audibly, and ANOOSHKA's lying on her favorite flat rock. We take in her fingers trailing in the water, her bare legs, T-shirt rolled up, belly bared to the sun.

While holding on her absolutely still BODY, we hear crackling noises through the brush, twigs breaking. A SHADOW falls over her. She doesn't

move. DROPS of water start dripping onto her belly from an unknown source.

She looks up, expecting RAPHAEL, and we see that, against all odds, it's ORPHEUS. He has dealt with his drug addiction, realized that she's the only one for him, tracked her down, and is ready to commit to a lifetime of bliss. (She sees this all in his look. It's very French.) Before she can even speak, camera moves to the sky, the music rises, and credits sail against the blue, up there with a flock of birds.

27. Bye-Bye Bug

It's March, and we've made it through the worst of the winter. Raphael and Agnes are actually expanding their coupledom, so we've all been hitting the movies. I've seen enough formulaic crap to last an eternity.

Lately I've been playing with a new scene:

The Hollywood Vengeance Ending

ANOOSHKA'S ISLAND—DAY

A deep blue sky, one cloud drifting. We move lazily across the sky and then down and down, taking in the lush, wild surroundings of ANOOSHKA's secret island in the middle of the river: a tiny outcropping of purple and yellow flowers shielded by tough saplings. The river's rushing audibly, and ANOOSHKA sits with the drawing of Orpheus as a bug which he gave her in the maze, so long ago. She crumples the drawing and holds it poised above the swift-moving river.

CUT TO:

FANTASY SEQUENCE. Same location, only ORPHEUS is there now, kneeling beside her, whispering in her ear. ANOOSHKA's eyes are closed.

ORPHEUS: You mean so much to me....

He grows a little smaller.

ORPHEUS: You are a perfect angel, a messenger....

He grows smaller still, and his voice begins to get higher and whinier....

ORPHEUS: You know, this really means something, this is real....

ANOOSHKA's eyes snap open and she looks, with annoyance, at this three-foot-tall, funny-voiced creature standing beside her. He persists, shrinking by the minute, eyes turning buggy, hands growing little flylike suctioney things.

ORPHEUS (with insect voice): I think we could really love each other....

Now he's just making buzzy fly sounds and he shrinks to the size of a bug and buzzes at her neck and ANOOSHKA finally can't take it anymore and swats at her neck with a piece of paper.

CLOSE-UP of tiny ORPHEUS-FACED squashed bug on paper.

CUT TO:

ANOOSHKA dropping the bug drawing into the river. We watch the current swiftly take it away.

ANOOSHKA (VO): I know I littered. But sometimes a girl's gotta do what she's gotta do.

Credits fall in the river, which is crystal clear, a bright mirror of the sky, with a lone bird winging along its merry way. The bird unexpectedly swoops down and plucks the litter out of the river as the music swells with orchestral splendor.

28. Flying

Agnes in the grass

*I met a girl / I really loved her /
how much she'll never know*

—from "Space," © ORPHEUS XTIIMUSIC

When spring comes, I get sick of the DVDs and start to read. It's been raining a lot, and it's so nice to sink into a book. At first—trashy, easy stuff. Now—deeper works. I pick up a book of myths and reread Orpheus and Eurydice. So short and simple: Love. Snake. She dies. He seeks her.

Grabs her hand. Pulls her back. Turns and looks and she disappears.

"What do you think it really means?" I ask Agnes one afternoon. Her grandma's pretty much recovered, but we got into the habit of visiting on Sundays. She's napping, and we're on the front porch working our way through a plate of cookies that we supposedly baked for Benita. The rain's melting the last bits of ice in the garden. Surprised greens prick up through last year's rotted leaves. This morning I saw a purple crocus and thought it was a plastic toy; it's been so long since we've had color on the ground.

"You know, I'm about sick of talking about this." She shoves another cookie in her mouth, eating it angrily.

"I'm sorry," I say.

She touches my arm. "No, I'm sorry. It's just that I miss you. I haven't even been able to have any girlfriend talk with you about Raphael."

A lush breeze with the scent of warm soil comes up in the silence between us. "Ag, I am really sorry. Tell me everything."

"Later," she says. "Let's just put this Orpheus shit to rest."

Agnes says we should analyze the myth, using the technique they use to understand dreams. It always goes back to dreams with Agnes.

Okay, I say, what do I do?

She tells me to close my eyes. Now just imagine you are Orpheus.

So I close my eyes and climb into his head.

Okay, I'm in love with Eurydice, we're in love, it's all innocent and cool and then—bam—sex. Or knowledge. A big ole coil of DNA, to borrow from the diary of the unmentionable man. Whatever it is that sends us crashing down into humanworld.

She disappears, but it's not really her who disappears after sex; it's my fantasy of her.

It was such a good fantasy, I can't let it go.

So I go underground—not into the subway, you literal thang, but down deep inside myself, bargaining, pleading. I'll do anything to have that fantasy back in place, that beautiful imagined time with that beautiful imagined person.

Voilà—I have it.

I can feel it, I can hear it, just like I felt Orpheus's physicality, his touch, his body, I felt those things in his bed; that was real.

And I heard his voice, all the beautiful things he said to me, but as soon as I turn to really look at the situation, really check it out, the fantasy vanishes.

And why did Orpheus, of the myth, feel so compelled to turn and look? Maybe Eurydice wanted him to.

"So he turns to look at her," I tell Agnes. "And she disappears. But who says that's a bad thing?"

Exactamonde, says Agnes. Now you are talking.

My own life spins on with no dramatic conclusion. School ends. Summer begins. It's nearly a year since it happened, and in spite of everything, I still miss Orpheus. But not as much!

I've stopped wanting to find out exactly what's going on in his mind. Sometimes things are better unsaid.

One summer morning, I'm on my way out—to get some sun and bury his stupid black plastic lighter on my island. On second thought—does it deserve a ritual? And I definitely don't need his stuff corrupting my island. I toss it in the kitchen garbage, on top of last night's fish bones and potato peelings. Throw a newspaper on top of that, so eagle-eyed Ma doesn't ask if I'm smoking or something. I flash on the lighter's final destination—buried in some charred pile of rot, eternally burning against an apocalyptic backdrop. Sounds good to me!

On my island, lying on the rock in the sun. The air is so pure and gentle. The water is quiet. The sky is quieter. And even if it were empty—but it's not. Reality is bigger than any feeling. There's a bird flashing through the air, and another. Still more, floating on the light current. It's harder to fly if you come from a womb. I take a breath anyway and begin to remember their secrets.

Acknowledgments

SPECIAL THANKS TO SARA CROWE FOR CHANGING MY LIFE IN THREE DAYS; TO ELLEN LEVINE FOR REMEMBERING, KATHERINE TEGEN FOR BEING A SUPPORTIVE VISIONARY, JULIE HITTMAN FOR HER SENSITIVITY AND DEDICATION, HILARY ZARYCKY AND ALI SMITH FOR THEIR ROCK AND ROLL EYESIGHT AND JANET FRICK FOR HER LONG HOURS. GRATITUDE TO MY FATHER FOR PUTTING IT ALL IN PERSPECTIVE AND TO THE OTHER EARLY READERS—LAURIE OLIVER, JERICHA SENYAK, DANA FRASER, RACHEL HERNANDEZ, ALEX KAMIN, HAILEY PEARSON AND EMILY ROBERTS-NEGRON—FOR THEIR CARING AND TIME AND THE SUFFERING INFLICTED UPON THEM DURING ENFORCED TELEPHONE MARATHONS.

FOR ALL THE ILLUMINATIONS FROM FAMILY, A SHOWERING OF COLORED STARS ON BENITA; ZHENYA; JOSH, TAMAR, ANNA AND ISAIAH; AL AND HAIL; MANETTE AND BILL; JERICHA AND SIMKA AND MS. SAKI AND TAMAR PT. 2 AND BIG MANETTE.

APPRECIATION FOR THE SMALL AND LARGE KINDNESSES OF THE RUHES— DOUG, JAMAL, SHAMSI AND THE PUGE; ROBBIE DUPREE; BOBBY GLAZER; DONNA HEIDER; ZIA AND AISHLING; PEP; DANA AND STEPHEN; ERNIE SHAW; PETER HEDGES; LINDA AND DIMITRI; LEA AND PHILIPPE; TIM, EUPHEMA AND TREVOR; BOBBY AND NINA; DONALD AND RICHARD.

AND FOR THE KINGS AND QUEENS OF COPIES AND SUNDRIES, HAIR AND CARS: ROB SHEAR; LOUISE ALLEN; DANIEL EASTON AND ARTHUR VOGEL.

THANKS TO DONNA OSZUST AND HER ENTIRE FAMILY, WHO LOVE TAJ TO PIECES AND FEED HIM STEAK. THANKS TO PEMA, KNUT AND NADJA.

AND FOR YOUR SONGS.

The invisible ones

some bruises go so deep
they never rise to the surface
can't you make that leap
to the solitary circus

some bruises go so deep
they never rise to the s
can't you make t

www.orpheusobsession.com